Bug Out! California
Book 9
Patriots United

Robert Boren

South Bay Press

Robert Boren

Book Layout ©2017 BookDesignTemplates.com
Cover Design: SelfPubBookCovers.com/Acapellabookcoverdesign
Bug Out! California Book 9/ Robert Boren. -- 1st ed.
ISBN:9781718049895

For Kent G.

There are no constraints on the human mind, no walls around the human spirit, no barriers to our progress except those we ourselves erect.
−Ronald Reagan

Contents

Previously, in Bug Out! California Book 8:

As Book 8 opened, Jules's group of battle wagons attacked an enemy communications center, but were surprised by M-60 tanks, which destroyed Gil and Tisha's rig, killing them both. They also attacked Cody and Allison's rig, rendering it useless. The team blew up the tanks with TOW missiles and escaped, leaving the communications installation in ruins.

In Dulzura, Ji-Ho realized that the enemy planned to re-open I-8 for Islamists heading north from Mexico. Sam and Ji-Ho's group was under almost constant attack, fending off the enemy but taking losses. They learned of a UN target in nearby Jamul, a staging area for new UN leadership, who were to be moved north to a new UN facility at an abandoned auto mall in Elk Grove. Sam and his team began planning an attack, coordinating with Ivan's team in the north, who were planning to hit the Elk Grove site shortly afterward.

On the way out of his hideout in San Francisco, Ivan set up a booby trap, leaving a body, a fedora and a pinstripe suit smeared with his DNA to fake his own death. The UN received tips about Ivan's location and rushed to the high-rise, breaking into Ivan's offices. The booby trap went off, killing the UN Peacekeepers and fooling the media into reporting that Ivan was killed.

Ivan learned that the UN was bringing captive women to the Elk Grove auto mall to entertain dignitaries. Mister White and Mister Black set up the attack, with the priority on protecting and rescuing the captive women.

The operation in Jamul was a success, Sam's team killing all the UN operatives. At the same time, UN Peacekeepers and Islamists were moving to attack Dodge City, but were stopped on the road by Garrett's cavalry.

As the time for the Elk Grove operation approached, Ivan revealed that Jules's next job would be at Folsom Prison. Surviving members of the California State Government were being held there. Ivan planned to spring them and put them back into place in Sacramento.

The operation in Elk Grove started, the captive women protected right from the start, as Ivan's commandos rushed into the facility, killing UN Peacekeepers by the dozen. Some Peacekeepers tried to leave the building and flee in their vans, but were killed by the battle wagons which had surrounded the building. Ivan set up for a TV shoot at the scene, which would include testimony by Morgan and the other women who had been held captive in the Torrance Police Station. Some of the women liberated at Elk Grove volunteered to join the TV broadcast as well. The UN appeared with tanks and Gaz Tigrs as the TV shoot was finishing, the battle wagons outside taking them on, with help from commandos on the roof, using M60s and TOW missile launchers. Jules and Ivan had another surprise for the enemy— several hundred armed off-roaders with M-19 grenade launchers mounted, using the gimbals designed by Curt in Texas. As the battle raged, the off-roaders flooded onto the scene from underground parking lots, cleaning up the remaining enemy fighters as the battle wagons picked up the hostages. Jules's team got away clean. The video for the TV broadcast was edited together with closed-circuit video of the Elk Grove facility and the battle. Ivan planned to break into all California TV channels again, after the Folsom Prison breakout was finished.

While the Dulzura away team was coming home from the Jamul operation, a massive enemy attack was launched at the Williams Place. The two battle wagons, the black-powder cannons, and the cavalry fought valiantly, but there were too many Islamists and UN Peacekeepers, all of them with modern weapons. They were on the verge of losing as Sam and his team arrived with their battle wagons, turning the tide of the battle. In a meeting afterwards, the team decided to abandon the Williams Place for Dodge City, which was easier to defend. They planned to leave right away, making several trips to move everyone during the late afternoon and early evening.

Ivan's video hit the airwaves and went viral on the internet. At the same time, unrest hit a tipping point in several Northern California cities, San Francisco and Oakland being the worst. Street battles exploded, patriots defeating the already weakened UN, taking the cities back. The enemy sent reserves from Folsom Prison to help, weakening their presence there. Ivan's intel team saw this, and told Jules to leave for the prison immediately.

Daan Mertins packed up his team and fled San Francisco, telling Saladin to head for Southern California, to help with the battle to re-open I-8. Daan also mentioned that the EU Navy ships carrying another sixty-thousand UN Peacekeepers were being diverted north to Oregon.

Seth was asked to develop an RFID history application, which would show movement of RFID hits, and would make it obvious when shielded vehicles were used to hide enemy movement. Aided by access to the high-res PC version of the

RFID apps provided by General Hogan, Seth set to work. This new app would become a crucial tool.

The Folsom Prison operation went well, and forty surviving California State Government officials were freed, taken to Sacramento in prison buses. Jules's rig was knocked over by a nearby explosion of an enemy ammo dump, giving him a mild concussion, but the team got away safely.

Dodge City was attacked with mortars, Islamists using a shielded van to hide their RFID chips. Garrett, Sid, Yvonne, and Tyler put down the attack quickly, and passed the word about the shielded van to Ivan. Sam warned that the attack was a test, and that they should expect a larger attack using shielded vehicles in the near future.

The California officials made it safely back to Sacramento, most of them not understanding what happened to the state while they were locked up. They bickered until Mr. White showed them how many Islamists were still in California. That and some discussion led them to understand what the situation was, and they started planning a counter-offensive.

In Bend, Oregon, a small group of young patriots were watching the EU Navy ship as it headed towards Portland. They were experts with social media, and had been recruiting like-minded people on a small level, hoping to join the coming battle of Portland with a force of several hundred. Portland was locked down with martial law, the city and state governments complicit, violent leftist activists ruling the streets like Nazi thugs of the 1930s. One of the Bend group had been on Ben Dover's recruitment site, and took advantage of its affiliate page, setting up a Central Oregon charter group. They used it to recruit people locally, but another member, who had connections to the

Portland music scene, helped get the recruitment links into that community.

Robbie was on the high-res app, watching a line of Islamist RFID hits heading into California from Nevada on I-80. They were spaced out, trying to hide their numbers. He wondered where they were going, and noticed a few stray hits in Sacramento, right next to the state headquarters of the CHP, which had recently re-formed after the release of the California legislators. Robbie notified Jules and Tex, who came over with Sparky. Jules called Ivan, who told them to go to the CHP headquarters immediately. Ivan mentioned that the CHP officers at the headquarters had been given M60s and M4s, and said he'd let them know what was coming so they could set up an ambush. The team fired up their battle wagons and took off, the off-roaders joining them. The action started right as they arrived, the enemy trying to set up mortars to pound the CHP headquarters, CHP officers on the roofs wailing away with M60s, the battle wagons and off-roaders getting into the battle.

In Bend, the affiliate recruiting link on Ben Dover's page was going viral. The number of recruits went from six-hundred to over eighty thousand in a short period of time, and was still rising fast. The Bend locals saw that most of the recruits were coming from Portland. Worried that the band web sites publishing recruitment links for the Bend group might be targeted, they called, not getting answers from any of them. One of the group reminded everybody that if the enemy had the phones of the band contacts, they now knew who tried to call them, which put the Bend patriots into a panic. They packed, getting ready to take off before they were captured by the State Police or worse.

Robert Boren

The battle for the CHP headquarters ended, the enemy losing all their fighters. Jules's group met with the CHP brass. The building where the three stray RFID hits showed up was across the street from the CHP building. They decided to search the building, using special forces men only. Jules, Tex, Ted, and Sparky all had such experience and volunteered. The CHP lead accepted and provided two of his men who had similar experience to join them. They were walking to the building as Book 8 came to an end...

The Patriots of Bend

Tex was leading a small force to the apartment building across the street from the CHP headquarters in Sacramento. Jules, Ted, and Sparky followed, along with CHP Officers Teter and Goldberg. The building was pockmarked with bullets, a few residents coming out, more driving in to survey the damage, having left when the gunfire started.

"Who's gonna clean this up?" Sparky asked. Tex shot him a smirk as they neared the door to the lobby.

"Where enemy bodies?" Jules asked.

"Fourth floor," Goldberg said. "Middle of the building. *Room 405.*"

"Is it over?" asked an old woman, standing on the sidewalk with a cart full of belongings.

"Yes, but we're going to check for any enemy fighters who might still be alive," Officer Teter said. "Please stay out here until we've given the all clear."

"Yes sir," she said. "Thank you."

The group went into the front door. "Want to check out their apartment first?" Goldberg asked.

"Might as well," Ted said. "Stairs."

"Yeah," Sparky said. Teter led them to the stairwell and they raced up, winded at the top.

"I need to be in better shape," Jules said, huffing and puffing.

"You and me both, boss," Sparky said.

They followed Teter down the walkway to the room, the door hanging open. "Watch yourselves. We killed these guys as the battle was raging. I'm assuming we got them all, but you never know."

Jules nodded, and the group went into the building in two-by-two formation, aiming their M4s as they searched, getting to the living room which opened onto a balcony facing the CHP building. The bodies were there, lifeless, staring into space.

Tex and Sparky rushed over, kneeling next to them, checking their pockets.

"What are you guys looking for?" Goldberg asked.

"Car keys," Tex said. "Bingo." He stood up, key fob in his hand. Sparky was checking the last body.

"Nothing in the rest," Sparky said. "Looks like the UN Peacekeeper was the driver."

"What kind of key is that?" Goldberg asked.

"*Mercedes*," Tex said, tossing the key fob to him.

"UN van," Jules said. "Wonder if marked?"

"I suspect we'll find out in a minute," Ted said. "Let's go to the parking garage."

"Wonder where the residents of this apartment are?" Sparky asked. "Look at the décor. This was an old person, or maybe an old couple."

"You're right," Goldberg said. "Looks like my grandma's place."

"You check the closets for bodies?" Tex asked.

"We checked them for hiding enemy fighters," Teter said. "Would've seen bodies. Nada."

"Okay, let's go," Ted said. The men left the building, Tex going slowly, falling behind as he looked at the floor of the walkway.

"C'mon, Tex, while we're young," Ted said.

"Hold it," Tex said, looking at a small smudge of blood that turned into a thin trail, going into the next unit.

"What?" Jules asked, looking at the spot he was staring at. "Uh oh."

"Yeah, uh oh," Tex said, walking towards the door as the others gathered around. He stood to the side of it and knocked hard. No answer.

Teter and Goldberg glanced at each other, then approached, not standing in front of the door, but off to the side as Tex was doing. Goldberg pounded on the door.

"Highway Patrol," he shouted. "Open up!"

Silence.

"Let's kick it in," Tex said.

Goldberg nodded. "Yeah, I think you're right."

"I've got it," Teter said, his massive leg kicking the door, breaking it open with the first try. The men got back into formation and slipped inside, aiming their rifles as they went.

"Oh, God," Teter said, lowering his weapon. The living room floor was covered with bodies, a mixture of elderly, middle aged, and children, all with their throats cut.

"They must've killed everybody on this floor," Sparky said, turning away from the carnage.

"Well, this side of the building, anyway," Goldberg said. "Those sick bastards."

"Time for us to take out the trash," Teter said, fire in his eyes. "Can't wait to kill more of these thugs."

"Let's check garage," Jules said. "Afterwards send CHP officers to search entire building. This might not be only dead people around."

Goldberg nodded in agreement, and the men went to the stairwell, taking it down to the underground garage.

"We'd better be careful when we go in here," Sparky said.

"Yeah, back into formation, guys," Ted said.

The men got their guns to their shoulders, and Teter opened the door, holding it as the others hurried through. He followed them. Goldberg took out the key fob and pushed the unlock button. There was a click and headlights went on, around the corner from where they were.

"Over there," Tex said. They rushed around the corner, staying in formation, their footsteps echoing in the cavernous garage.

"There," Sparky said. "UN van without the insignia."

"Just what I expect," Jules said. The men trotted to it, guns still up.

Teter led the way, getting next to the side sliding door. "Get ready." He grabbed the door handle and opened it. Everybody's short range app went off, and a gunshot sounded. Jules opened fire, killing the lone Islamist before he could hit anybody.

"Son of a bitch, look at the inside of this sucker," Tex said, sticking his head in. "Lead, lining the entire inside."

"So, UN creeps drive, others in shielded back compartment," Jules said. "This bad development, no?"

"How many could they have?" Ted asked. "Lead in this amount is hard to come by, and they could only shoehorn about eight fighters in here, max. They'd need hundreds of semi-trailers set up like this to field a usable force."

"I call Ivan," Jules said. "We might not be only team that see this."

"Yeah, partner, you do that," Tex said.

***

Jonathan was driving his battered pickup truck east on Oregon Boulevard, the Bend traffic sparse for a late afternoon. Courtney was in the passenger seat, eyes on her phone. She looked up.

"Why are we going this way? We hitting Jared's place?"

Jonathan shot her a worried glance. "I want to make sure he's leaving. He didn't answer my last text."

"Maybe we better split. They might be looking for us right now."

"They might," Jonathan said. "Wish we had one of the long guns up here."

"They'll throw us in jail if they catch us with a gun up here."

"They'll throw us in jail if they catch us, period," Jonathan said, "once we get out of Bend, anyway."

"You don't think the local cops would bust us?"

"No," Jonathan said. "I know all of them. They're on our side. They know what's happening with the EU ship full of UN Peacekeepers. I think some of them will join us."

They rounded the bend, getting onto Hawthorne Avenue.

"Look, roadblock, just past Hill Street," Courtney said.

"Oregon State Police," Jonathan said. "Dammit."

"They're not on our side?"

"Nope," Jonathan said, slowing to a stop and parking on the curb, half a block from Hill Street.

"They're gonna see us," Courtney said, getting lower in her seat.

"No they aren't. They're all watching Jared's house. They've got assault rifles pointing at it."

"We need to go," Courtney said.

"In a minute," Jonathan said, pulling his phone out. He sent a text.

"What are you doing?"

"I'm letting Officer Peterson know that there's three State Police cars at Jared's house," Jonathan said. His phone dinged with a reply.

"Well?"

"They're already on the way," Jonathan said, "with most of the force."

Courtney looked shocked. "They're going to fight the State Police?"

"They don't want to be replaced by the UN," Jonathan said. "They understand what's going on."

Suddenly four Bend Police cruisers raced by them on the tree-lined street, crashing through the barricades, as several more raced up the street from the other direction. Armed officers leapt out of their vehicles.

"Oh, shit," Cortney said.

Jonathan watched, his heart racing. "This is gonna be bad."

One of the State Police officers came out with a bull horn. "Stop right there. This is out of your jurisdiction."

"Stand down now!" yelled one of the Bend Police officers.

"We aren't going to tell you again," the man with the bull horn said. "We're here under the authority of the Governor of Oregon."

"Screw you," the police officer shouted back. "We won't allow the UN to come in here. No way in hell. Stand down or be fired upon."

Several State Police officers pointed their guns at the Bend Police, all of whom pulled their weapons.

"Hold your fire," the State Police officer said.

"Stand down immediately," the Bend Officer shouted again.

Suddenly one of the State Police officers fired, hitting the Bend Officer. The first State officer dropped his bullhorn and looked at the dead man in terror, then turned to yell at the officer who fired. It was too late. Gunfire erupted from the Bend police, all the State Police officers in sight dropping, most of them dead.

"Son of a bitch," Jonathan shouted.

"No!" Courtney said. They watched as Bend officers rushed into the duplex. Gunfire could be heard from inside, then silence.

"Geez," Jonathan said. He watched as the Bend officers came out the front door, followed by Jared and several of his friends.

"Well, they're still alive," Courtney said. "They're rounding up the State Police officers that are still alive."

Jonathan sent another text. They could see an officer pull his phone and look at it. He typed on his phone, then turned towards their truck and motioned them over.

"C'mon," Jonathan said, opening his door. His phone dinged with the text.

"You sure? What if more state cops show up?"

"There's enough of our guys here to blast them," he said, going to the truck bed. He opened the camper shell and grabbed his Mini-14.

"What are you doing?" Courtney asked.

"Officer Jenkins said to bring it."

"Why, so they can take it away from you?"

"Don't worry about it," Jonathan said. "C'mon."

The two trotted over to the group of officers.

"Hey, Jonathan," said Officer Jenkins, a man no older than him. "Thanks for giving us the heads up."

"No problem," Jonathan said. "Jared!"

Jared looked over and smiled, his right eye blackened, scrapes on his cheeks. "Hey, dude."

"What happened to you?" Courtney asked, staring at his battered face.

"The Oregon State Gestapo," Jared said, shrugging. "I didn't get out fast enough."

The radio in Jenkin's car blipped. He rushed over and got it, then came back just as quickly. "They're at your place now, Jonathan. You can't go back there."

"That means they'll be here any minute," Courtney said.

"You guys going with us to Portland?" Jared asked.

"We were," Officer Jenkins said. "Now we're gonna set up roadblocks to keep the State Police away from Bend. We could use volunteers. Want to be deputized? I think a hundred thousand patriots in Portland is enough."

"Deputize us?" Jared asked. "What is this, the old west?"

Officer Jenkins laughed. "We can still do it, and this is at least as wild as the *Wild West* now. Gonna get worse before it gets better."

"Wait a minute," said an older man with a lieutenant's uniform on, walking over. "You sure these guys are okay?"

"I'll vouch for them, sir," Jenkins said. "Known them all my life."

"I was kinda looking forward to taking on the UN and the EU Navy," Jared said.

The lieutenant studied him for a moment, then shook his head, shooting a side-long glance at Jenkins. "You're sure?"

"Yes sir," Jenkins said. "I know others too. In my gun club, for instance."

"Okay, go ahead and recruit them," he said, turning to Jared. "Look, son, there's a difference to be made *here*. I suspect if you tried to go to Portland, you'd be shot on the way in."

"We can't let the UN Peacekeepers get a foothold," Jared said.

"And they won't," the Lieutenant said. "My brother and sister are both in Portland. There's more people getting involved than you know. It's more like two hundred thousand now, and most of the city officials who put martial law in place have gone into hiding. All they have left now is the State Police, and not all of them are towing the line. We're gonna take this state back, but we need to protect our family and our home. You're here now and can make a difference. Stay and help us."

"You guys can work recruitment for us," Jenkins said. "You've proven yourselves to be good at that, you know."

The lieutenant nodded in agreement. One of the other officers rushed over and whispered in his ear. He thanked the officer and picked up the bull horn from next to the dead State Police officer, putting it to his lips. "Find some cover and get ready. State Police and some of their friends are on the way here right now."

"Friends?" Jonathan asked. The lieutenant ignored the question as he rushed off to attend to some other officers.

"C'mon," Jenkins said. "They'll head in here on Bend Parkway again."

"I'd be ready for them to show up from any direction," Jared said. "Gotta go get my weapon." He ran off to the rear of his building.

"What should I do?" Courtney asked.

"Get in the basement of Jared's duplex," Jonathan said.

"No way, I'm gonna fight," she said, "so get used to that. I saw what those women said on the video."

"This is why I love you," Jonathan said.

Her eyes grew wide. "You love me? You've never said that before. Hell, *I've* never said that before."

He smiled, pulling her in for a kiss, then getting back and looking at her. "I'm not the greatest communicator. You know that. Let's go to the truck. You can use the 20-gauge pump. I've got about four boxes of shells for that sucker, and it doesn't kick too hard."

"I've shot it before, remember?"

"Yeah, you were better than me at the skeet range," Jonathan said, taking her by the hand and running to the truck. They grabbed the shotgun and shells, and more ammo for the mini-14. When they got back, Jared was there with a couple more friends, all of them holding M4 variants. They took up positions along the end of Hawthorne Street where it met Hill street, but there weren't enough good spots.

"Hey, how about those box cars over there?" Jonathan asked, pointing at them on the tracks across Hill Street.

"Perfect, but make sure you don't get seen from the back side," Jenkins said.

Jonathan, Courtney, Jared, and several others rushed over there, getting behind the cars and underneath them, guns aimed up and down the street. State police squad cars and white vans came into view.

"Look, that's about twenty vehicles," Jared said. "What's with the vans? Never seen them before."

"Look at the sides," Courtney said, squinting to read. "Says UN in blue letters."

"Shit, they're in Bend already?" Jonathan asked.

"They must've been infiltrating us for a while," Jared said. "Here they come. Lock and load."

"Don't try to hit them with the shotgun until they're real close," Jonathan said. "Better yet, save it for when they get out of their vehicles and start running."

"I know," Courtney said, as she fed shells into the gun's loading gate.

Gunfire erupted from the other side of the street, hitting the first of the State Police cruisers, stopping them in their tracks. The other vehicles stopped in a panic, trying to get out as a hail of lead came at them.

"Get those vans!" Jonathan shouted. "It's the UN!"

Now everybody was firing, the fronts of all the vehicles getting hit. The side doors of the UN vans opened, men running out towards them. Courtney smiled at Jonathan, then turned and fired, hitting running men one after another until they figured out they'd better take cover.

"C'mon, let's go towards them from behind the box cars," Jared said. "Maybe we can get behind them."

"Good idea," Jonathan said. They ran behind the boxcars in a crouch, getting all the way to Irving Avenue.

"This is good," Jared whispered. "See them over there?"

The three got down on their bellies and opened fire, the UN Peacekeepers and State Police officers looking for cover in a panic, not even trying to return fire. Courtney fired her shotgun with deadly accuracy, dropping several more enemy officers.

The remaining UN Peacekeepers bolted and ran, Jonathan and Jared picking them off before they got twenty yards.

"I think it's over," Jonathan whispered, eyes scanning the area. Courtney was doing the same, taking a moment to top up her magazine with shells. Jenkins and several other Bend officers were coming down the street now, rushing from one bit of cover to the next, checking the vehicles.

"Is it all clear?" Jared shouted.

"Stay under cover," one of the officers yelled as he moved forward. A shot rang out, and he dived behind a car, the fire returned from all the cops in the street along with Jonathan and the others by the tracks. Courtney saw several men get up to run, so she bolted forward, firing her shotgun as she ran, dropping several more, Jonathan after her, looking in all directions for more enemy fighters. There was silence for a few moments. Courtney got out of the crouch she was in and walked back towards Jonathan, a smile on her face. Then another shot rang out, and her expression changed. She crumpled to the street. Jonathan saw the UN Peacekeeper who shot her and fired, hitting him square in the chest, then rushing over to Courtney.

Her eyes were still open, a faint smile coming over her face as she saw him above her. "I got a little of our own back," she said softly. "I nailed seven of them."

"Don't talk," Jonathan said, his tears dropping onto her face as he watched her.

"I love you too," Courtney whispered. Her body spasmed, and she exhaled, dying as he watched.

"Oh, no!" Jonathan cried, kissing her forehead, cradling her body as their friends looked on.

{2}

The Battle of Portland

A huge crowd of radicals ringed the Swan Island Basin in Portland, Oregon, many with signs, most wearing all black with masks covering their faces below the eyes. Behind them were several hundred Portland PD officers in riot gear, attempting to stay between them and a growing number of counter-protesters.

Nathan watched the water nervously as the big EU Navy ship cruised slowly towards the dock. He turned every few seconds to watch the counter-protesters, holding American flags and signs that said NO UN. He was only twenty-five, medium build, tattoos covering his upper arms and neck, large round earrings stretching his lobes.

"Hey, Sean," he said quietly. "This makes me nervous. There's only one way out of here, and that's more counter protesters than I've ever seen before. Why is the Portland PD letting them get so close?"

Sean's eyes turned his direction, his cheeks rising under his black bandana, eyes smaller as he laughed. "Rednecks and retired people. I'm gonna break some heads as soon as the UN Peacekeepers show themselves." He was smaller than Nathan, holding a long stick with finishing nails sticking out a few inches on either end, his medium-length blonde hair shining in the sun.

"I'm hearing bad rumors," Nathan said, looking back at the ship as it slowly moved towards the dock, a crew there to grab the ropes. A UN flag rose on the flagpole over the bridge, and a cheer went up from a few thousand black-clad people.

"Watch those old Nazis crap themselves when the UN Peacekeepers come down the planks," Sean said.

"The reactionaries outnumber the police now," Nathan said. "At least two to one, and they're still showing up."

"And we've got sixty thousand UN Peacekeepers getting off that boat," Sean said. "You worry too much. As soon as we get rough with those old cupcakes, they'll turn tail and run… and even if they don't we'll be protected by the police as usual."

"The public is starting to see through this, you know."

"So go home, little boy," Sean said.

"Hey, we'd better get out of here!" cried a woman in black with a mask, her stringy brown hair hanging around her shoulders. "Look at this."

"Shut up, Emily," Sean said.

"What do you see?" Nathan asked, rushing over. She held her phone in front of him. It was news-chopper video of the area. There was a vast multitude of people heading in on all streets, crossing North Willamette Boulevard. "My God. How many people is that?"

"Let me see it," Sean said, rushing over and looking. He laughed. "You guys are assuming that they're not on our side." Emily and Nathan looked at him like he was crazy.

"We know the community," Emily said. "If there was this many people coming, we'd have known about it days ago."

"Well run along home, then," Sean said, turning back to the ship. It was tied to the dock now, and the gang plank was being rolled up.

"Oh, God," Emily said, looking at her phone again. "Is that another warship. See it? Just getting to Kelley Point Park."

"There's more than one ship in the EU Navy, you idiot," Sean said, looking over at the counter protesters again. Several black-clad thugs were rushing past the police line, attacking counter protestors as the police stood by and watched. Suddenly the number of counter demonstrators increased and the police loudspeaker warned all the protestors to go back to their sides. Sean ran towards them as Nathan and Emily watched.

"Moron," Emily said. "Want to go? No paycheck is worth this."

"Dressed like this, we'll never make it past Willamette," he said. "C'mon, let's jump the box factory fence and get on one of the semi-trailers in the yard. We can watch from there, then slip out in the confusion."

Emily glanced towards the box factory. "Okay." They pushed their way towards the fence as most of the black-clad thugs headed to the counter-protester lines. Police began to fire tear gas at the growing crowd of citizens, ignoring the thugs who raced in and attacked them.

Nathan climbed the fence, turning when he was on the far side to help Emily up. They both hit the pavement of the box factory lot and raced towards the row of semi-trailers parked at the loading docks.

"There's one we can get on," Nathan said, racing towards it, Emily struggling to keep up. He leapt onto a dumpster next to one of them, and jumped, getting a good hand hold and pulling himself up on top. "C'mon, I'll grab you."

Emily looked at him, scared to death, frozen in place.

"Now, dammit!" Nathan shouted.

She snapped out of it and ran, jumping onto the dumpster, taking Nathan's hand. He pulled her up, and they both stood.

"Holy crap," Emily said, watching the hand-to-hand fighting between the black-clad people, citizens wearing casual clothes, and police, who were firing bean bags at the counter protestors now.

"Look, UN Peacekeepers!" Nathan said, pointing. "They're coming down the gang plank in a hurry! That'll show the reactionaries."

Emily turned to Nathan, horrified. "They're lining the deck with their guns out."

"Show of force," Nathan said. "Good. That battle is getting out of hand."

"Our people are getting the crap beat out of them," Emily said, watching as more and more citizens rushed in, trampling the protesters, kicking them and punching them as they tried to fight back with their clubs, sticks, pepper spray, and bags of urine.

"Look, the police are running away," Nathan said. "Son of a bitch. What are they doing? There's still too many counter-protesters here!"

"Damn Mayor's office. This is complete lack of coordination."

Suddenly gunfire erupted from the deck of the ship, UN Peacekeepers firing into the fighting crowd, hitting the black-clad people and counter-protesters alike.

"No!" Emily shouted, watching people falling to the ground. Then there were screams and yells as the area flooded with thousands of armed citizens, taking aim with their rifles and firing at the ship, killing several of the Peacekeepers as the rest dropped behind cover in shocked horror. Automatic fire started up from several groups of citizens, bullets hitting the gang plank, knocking down the Peacekeepers who were trapped there.

"Those are military weapons!" shouted Nathan. "I see M60s and M-16s! Where'd they get those?"

"You know how those white nationalists are," Emily said, tears running down her cheeks.

"They can't own those," Nathan said. "Somebody gave those guns to them for this event."

"Those sailors are uncovering the weapons on the boat," Emily said, her eyes wide as they opened fire on the crowd, strafing with machine gun fire. One of the citizens with an M60 fired back, hitting the men behind one gun, another gunner hitting the man. Several more citizens with M60s rushed up, firing from behind cover now. The UN Peacekeepers were back, firing, hitting citizens, but also taking fire from every direction around the dock, many of them hit.

"This is horrible," Nathan said.

"Here comes that other boat," Emily said. "Shit, that's a US Navy ship!"

Just as the words left her lips, several missiles were fired, all of them hitting the EU ship, blowing the top half of it to pieces, silencing the machine gun fire. A cheer rang out from the multitude, sounding like a huge roar.

"We'd better get out of here," Emily said.

"Take off that outfit," Nathan said, pulling off his black shirt.

"I can't, I don't have anything on underneath."

"Look, there's more of them," shouted an old man holding an M-16, leading a group of citizens onto the box factory lot. Those were the last words Emily and Nathan heard.

***

Daan looked out his tenth-floor apartment window, at a quiet night in Brussels. He had more work to do. The UN refused to continue pumping men and materiel to the United States without additional funding, and the EU leadership refused to do anything. His cellphone rang. It was the UN Secretary General. He let it go to voicemail, then walked to his bar and poured himself some whiskey. Leverage. *He needed leverage.* His phone rang again. *Dammit.* He looked. *Saladin.* His heart pounded.

"Hello," he said as he sat on his couch.

"Still in Brussels?" Saladin asked.

"Yeah, but I'll be coming back soon."

"Have you seen the news, or talked to any of the team?" Saladin asked.

"Oh, shit, what happened now?"

"We had a really bad day on several fronts," Saladin said.

"Can't be much worse than what's happened here," Daan said. He drank down his whiskey and went to get another, leaning against his bar. "Let's have it."

"We sent a team to take out the CHP headquarters in Sacramento. They were defeated."

"Dammit. By whom?"

"Ivan's people in their blasted motor homes and off-roaders, and about sixty CHP officers. Somebody armed them with military weapons. They knew we were coming. Like I suspected, they broke your RFID chips."

"That remains to be seen. They had to expect we'd try to hit the CHP before they could get rolling. All the leadership was there, and it's a state-wide organization."

Saladin chuckled. "So why did you okay that operation, then?"

"Hey, it was your idea, remember?"

Saladin was silent for a moment, his breath quickening on the mouthpiece.

"Sorry," Daan said. "Don't get pissed. We both thought it was a good idea."

"Fine," Saladin said, an icy tone to his voice. "There's more."

"All right, let's hear it," Daan said.

"This one should be all over the news, especially there, so I'll tell you the gist, and you can see the details yourself."

"Go ahead," he said.

"The EU ship bringing UN Peacekeepers to Portland was destroyed by a US Navy Aegis Cruiser. All our assets were killed, including the Peacekeepers, the sailors on the vessel, and many of our domestic operatives. Oh, and most of our people in the city leadership were rounded up and shot as well."

Daan felt faint, gripping the bar. He moved to a stool and sat, leaning his head in his hands.

"You still there?" Saladin asked.

"Yeah." He poured another drink. "That means we can write off that state."

"I agree," Saladin said. "There was also action in Bend and several other of the inland cities. We lost in each location."

"How?"

"Ivan's social media operation," he said.

"Ben Dover," Daan said. "We need to kill him. Make it a priority."

"He's in the middle of territory we no longer control. We've lost the top third of the state."

"Dammit, we also lost LA and Orange Counties. What do we still control?"

"We don't control *any* of California," he said.

"You mean we should leave the state? Is there anywhere that the locals don't control?"

"They don't have control of the area from Merced south to about I-15. We still operate there, but it would be an exaggeration to say we *controlled* it."

"Crap, there's nothing there," Daan said.

"Yes, there is. Much of their best agriculture is there, also their oil fields."

"Yeah, whatever," he said.

"The agriculture is more important than you think," Saladin said. "Remember that the lines of trade aren't in place now."

"Except for that little body of water called the Pacific Ocean," Daan said.

"The EU Navy is still strong off the coast."

"And yet we allowed a US Navy ship to cruise right in and destroy one of our boats," Daan said. "The parts of Southern California other than LA and Orange Counties are still in contention, are they not?"

"We are still active and powerful enough in those areas to keep working, but we must get that southern route opened back up. I-8 and the others. Everything depends on it."

"On that we agree," Daan said. "Is your caravan still proceeding south?"

"Yes, but I have them well spaced out, so they'll attract as little attention as possible. We're still hitting at Ivan's people down there. They think they have a safe place, but we attacked them there a few days ago. If we can force them to get on the move again, we'll start to pick them off."

"Those forces that caused us so many problems up north are still around," Daan said. "What if they come south too?"

"We should try to slip people north to take it back over. I could bring a lot of people in through Nevada."

"Won't that hurt your campaign against General Hogan?"

"Temporarily," Saladin said, "but I no longer consider that as important as I did before."

"Why not?"

"Like I was saying, they cracked your RFID chips. That makes Frank Johnson a less important target than before."

"I still want him," Daan said. "I'll roast him alive, but I'm not ready to accept that he's broken the RFID encryption. If he's done that, we'd lose all our assets in Washington DC. You know that, right? If those people are safe, we can assume that the RFID encryption is still protecting us."

"Is it possible that they only broke part of the system?" Saladin asked.

"What do you mean?"

"Is it possible they can track location but not have access to the data payload?" Saladin asked.

"Oh. Possible but unlikely. The encryption of the device is just as rigorous as the encryption of the data payload."

"You don't sound convinced by your own statement," Saladin said.

"It's been a long day, and it's not over yet. Now I know why the UN Secretary General just tried to call me."

"He tried to call you? Just now? I didn't hear any beeps."

"No, before you called," Daan said. "I didn't want to talk to him. Now I don't have a choice."

"What happened back there?"

"The UN leadership dug in their heels on increased funding to stay in the fight, and the EU leadership refused to cough up more money."

Saladin laughed. "So, work it harder. You know how that goes."

"After what just happened, my job is even harder than before."

"Mine too, my friend, but we have to roll with the punches," Saladin said.

"All right," Daan said. "Anything else?"

"Fortunately, no," Saladin said. "Talk to you soon." He ended the call. Daan grabbed the bottle of whiskey and his glass, and headed for the couch. He hit the Secretary General's contact.

***

Seth and Kaitlyn sat at a table against the wall in the Dodge City Saloon. Most of their friends were up at the bar, having a drink and chatting.

"Go ahead," Kaitlyn said.

"What?"

"You brought the laptop for a reason. Plug it in and get it warmed up. Then you can monitor your new program while we're here."

"Okay," he said. "You can go hang with Megan and the others while I check, and I'll be along."

"I'm with the person I want to be with right now," she said, putting her hand on his arm. "Trust me. I'm interested in what your program is showing too, so fire it up. I'll go get you a beer if you want."

"Sure, that'd be great, as long as I just have one."

"Nobody's drinking a lot," Kaitlyn said as she slid out of her seat. "Be right back."

Seth put his laptop on the table and set it up, plugging it into a wall outlet next to him. After it was running, he took out his phone and activated the personal hot spot. The laptop connected, and Seth navigated to his server, hitting the report download button. Excel started, and his report populated after a couple minutes. Kaitlyn came back, holding two beers. He took his and had a sip.

"Not bad," he said.

"Yeah, I was pleasantly surprised," Kaitlyn said, sitting back down. "Is it still working?"

"Yep," he said. "I downloaded a report into Excel. You could probably help with this part."

"Let's see," she said, watching as he turned the laptop to face her. She studied it for a few minutes. "I see what you're doing here. I couldn't have done any better, honestly. Maybe I could automate more of it."

"You see any quadrants where we've had RFID chips disappear?"

She studied it again for a moment, eyes squinting, until she found the right column and understood what it was saying. "Yes, I do see something funny."

"Shit, really?" Seth asked, getting up and looking over her shoulder.

"Is that what this means?" she asked, moving the cursor over a column.

"I set it up so at least four had to disappear without them being someplace else."

"What if they just left?"

"It's looking at a hundred square miles," Seth said. "Unless they were right on the border of that, they couldn't move out of range fast enough. He took a closer look. "This one is okay. The text would show up red if the rules applied. These folks were close to the border."

"Can you move it to make sure?"

"Yeah, but I'll have to run the report again."

"Do it," she said. "I'm interested."

He nodded. "I'll show you how, in case we need it run and I'm not around." He walked her through the procedure, and they ran the report, covering the area nearest to where the missing hits were.

"That's them, isn't it?" she asked.

"Looks like it."

"We don't have a problem, then?"

"Not yet," Seth said.

"Why don't you look at a larger area?"

"It's harder to analyze."

"You see, that's where I can help," she said. "Let me mess with the reporting for a while. Can you set this to run for, say, a thousand square miles?"

"Sure, but it'll take a while to run."

"Dammit, I was due at the cinema in ten minutes," she said. Seth laughed, and she shot him a smirk. "Let me help you, okay?"

"Okay," Seth said. "You know how to set the scope. Adjust the settings and run it again."

"We won't have history for all of it, though, will we?"

"Nope, but we'll run it that way and gather the history," Seth said. "Mind if I watch you? I could use better knowledge of Excel."

"Be my guest," she said. He pulled up a chair next to her and watched as she worked.

3

Southern Routes

Jules finished backing the battle wagon under the massive cover structure at their base. The other rigs were doing the same, and off-roaders rushed into the big quarry's equipment lot like a swarm of hornets.

Shelly looked over at him, eyes sleepy. "We don't have a bunch of stuff to do, I hope? I'm so tired."

"Me too," Jules said as he shut down the engine. "I go do hook up. Get into bed, I'll join soon."

"Okay, honey," she said, getting out of the passenger seat and walking to the back of the rig.

Jules went out to hook up the power and water. Tex was doing the same on his rig in the next space.

"Hey, partner, you been listening to the news?"

"No, Tex, what I miss?" He opened his utility compartment.

"Portland. The EU Navy ship steamed up there, ready to unload sixty thousand UN Peacekeepers. There was a huge battle, with a couple hundred thousand patriots flooding the dock area."

"Oh, really?" Jules asked. He pulled out his power cable and plugged it into the mast, then flipped on the breaker. "Sounds like somebody was on social media."

"Probably," Tex said, pausing to connect his water. "It gets better. A US Navy ship was following it, and just as the EU ship was starting to use its weapons on the citizens, it got hit with three missiles. Blew up the ship and killed all the UN Peacekeepers."

"Gee, that too bad," Jules said, shooting Tex a wicked grin. "Bet Daan isn't happy right now."

"Of course, the news media is portraying this whole thing as a frigging tragedy, but bottom line is that the enemy has lost Oregon."

"That battle only, not war," Jules said.

Tex chuckled. "The citizens went on a rampage. They rounded up all of the crooked political hacks who put martial law in and shot them."

Jules froze. "Shot them? Maybe we do win there, then."

"The radio announcer was expressing hope that the EU or the UN will come in and install order."

"Yeah, we know what kind of *order* they talk, no?"

"Exactly," Tex said. "If this event didn't cause so much loss of life, they wouldn't have covered it, partner."

"They cover CHP hit?"

Tex laughed. "Nope. Thanks for making my point."

Both men cracked up. Ted walked over with Sparky.

"You guys talking about the Portland thing?" Ted asked.

"Yes, Tex just fill me in," Jules said.

"The worm has turned there," Sparky said. "Hopefully Seattle will be next."

"Bigger nut to crack," Jules said.

Robbie came over. "You guys talking about what happened up north?"

"Yes," Jules said. "You hear?"

"I had the radio on, caught the gist," Robbie said. "No need to go back over it, unless you have some inside info."

"Nope," Jules said.

"Something's on your mind, partner," Tex said.

"We got back a little before you guys did," Robbie said. "I've been back on that new high-res app. I think we're gonna get a flow of enemy fighters coming in from Nevada."

"Where do you see?" Jules asked.

"There's a well spread-out group coming from the Salt Lake City area, along I-80," Robbie said. "They weren't there before we left."

"Wonder if they want to take Oregon back?" Sparky asked.

"No way," Ted said. "If they were going to Oregon, they'd be going up I-84."

"There aren't enough people in Oregon for them to make that kind of move," Robbie said. "Not after we've whacked them so bad in the northern half of California."

"He smart," Jules said. "They lost top third of California, along with LA and Orange counties in south. They do two things. Send big forces south to open I-8, and try to take back Sacramento and Bay Area. They must do fast, too, or they have no chance."

"What about the battle with General Hogan?" Sparky asked.

"General Hogan forces retreat from Utah," Jules said. "Head for Kansas. Ivan told me. Maybe Saladin thinks Hogan is on run."

Tex took off his cowboy hat and scratched his head. "Something doesn't add up here. You think the enemy leadership is starting to lose it?"

"Maybe the enemy leadership figured out what my dad has done, and now killing him isn't the priority it once was," Robbie said. "The cat's already out of the bag."

"That possible," Jules said. "Still must defeat General Hogan forces to win war."

"They already know they're in trouble," Ted said. "This could be a Hail-Mary for California. How many troops are on the way, kid?"

"A lot," Robbie said. "They've spaced them out, like I said, but I'm seeing about two hundred thousand."

"Crap," Sparky said. "We need to get ready for this."

"Robbie, keep tracking," Jules said. "How far closest group?"

"None had passed the Utah border as of a few minutes ago," he said.

"That's good and bad," Ted said.

"What mean?" Jules asked.

"It could mean that there are more than two hundred thousand on the way," he said. "Some might not have left the huge base in Salt Lake City yet."

"Assuming no stop-overs to rest, that's nine hours," Tex said, looking at his phone.

"It's actually ten hours," Robbie said. "Remember the time-zone change."

"Oh, yeah," Tex said. "They aren't gonna drive straight through, though."

"Don't be so sure, they probably have more than one driver per vehicle," Ted said.

"I go call Ivan," Jules said. "Talk later. Robbie, keep up good work."

"Hey, partner, where are those Islamists that are headed south?" Tex asked.

Robbie turned back to him as he was walking away. "Settled in for the night. The group who's made it the furthest is in Warner Springs."

"Crap, they're going to link up with the big group in Julian, and go on a rampage," Tex said.

"Keep eye on that too," Jules said. "We won't be able to help as soon as I thought."

Jules left the others, climbing the steps into his rig.

"You coming to bed, honey?" Shelly asked from the bathroom.

"Soon, must call Ivan," he said. "New development."

"Good or bad development?"

"Not sure," Jules said, sitting on the couch. He pulled out his phone and hit Ivan's contact, then put it on speaker. It rang twice, and Ivan picked up.

"Jules, nice job at the CHP headquarters," Ivan said.

"Thanks, boss. Robbie see something. We should talk."

"Uh oh," Ivan said. "What?"

"Large group of Islamists heading west on I-80," Jules said. "Coming from Salt Lake City."

"We've been watching," Ivan said. "They haven't left Utah yet."

"Yes, that what Robbie say. What you think? Should we stick around up here?"

"I need more information," Ivan said. "We're working that now. We saw a mass of fighters rush into Salt Lake City; we thought they'd be heading to Oregon after what happened there."

"Oregon not worth squat," Jules said. "Only reason UN Peacekeepers go there is we shut down landing spot in Bay Area."

Ivan was silent for a moment. "We're starting to think the same thing. It's not a good development. We need you guys in the south. Ji-Ho and Sam have a firestorm coming their way, and they haven't the resources to handle it yet."

"You work recruitment, no?"

"Ben Dover's got a sub-team on it, but it's just getting started, and we'll have a harder time with weapons distribution than we had up north."

"Why?" Jules asked.

"Can't use San Diego port. It's controlled by the US Navy."

"They're on our side, no?"

"Yes, Jules, but they aren't advertising it, and their attitude is that any increase in distribution of weapons down there is likely to bite them in the ass. And by the way, they're right to worry. If Ji-Ho's team is destroyed, the weapons will be used to attack eastern San Diego county, and they'll work their way west quickly. Remember what the US Navy is dealing with now."

"EU Navy," Jules said. "Dammit."

"Don't worry, it's not all bad," Ivan said. "They've lost Oregon for good, provided they don't win the larger war in Texas, the southwest, and California."

"They have to win all three?" Jules asked.

"Yeah, and they'd have to get it done before the people in the mid-Atlantic, New England, and the upper Midwest throw off the yoke of martial law. The clock is running on that."

Jules chuckled. "Okay, when you put like that, not so bad."

"There's one other issue going on," Ivan said. "I've got only a sketchy account of this. I'm trying to get more info but we don't have much intelligence on the EU."

"You want me to put feelers out?"

"No, Jules, leave it alone for now. In a nutshell, the UN is pushing for more money to stay in the battle, in places like California, New England, and the Mid-Atlantic. The EU isn't budging on funding. They're already picking up the UN funding slack since the USA has pulled back."

"Daan is having nightmare over this, I bet."

"That's what we think," Ivan said. "We'll see what happens."

"Wish UN would pull back. No RFID makes them harder to deal with, even though they don't fight as well as the Islamists."

"One more thing, Jules, then I've got to go."

"Go ahead, boss."

"Ji-Ho's group got attacked by enemy troops using a shielded vehicle like you found in that parking garage next to the CHP headquarters."

"Really? How many snuck in?"

"Very few, in only one van, with UN Peacekeepers driving in the unshielded part of the cabin. Ji-Ho has a person looking for lead dealers in California who are making a lot of sales. We may want to have your data person chat with their data person. His name is Seth."

"You want Robbie to chat with him? Okay, we can make that happen. I send message to Ji-Ho to set up."

"You do that, Jules. Now rest a while, but have somebody watching the long-range app. Don't let the Islamists from Utah catch you with your pants down."

"Understand," Jules said. "Good bye."

The call ended. Shelly stuck her head out of the bathroom. "Interesting conversation."

"I turn up loud so you can hear," Jules said. "What doing in there so long?"

"Primping a little," she said. "Can we go to bed now?"

"Why rush?"

"I'm still in my fertile period, remember?" She came out of the bathroom wearing nothing but a smile.

"You don't have to ask twice," Jules said, following her into the bedroom.

***

It was quiet at Dodge City. Sam stepped out of the tiny shower in the battle wagon, reaching for a towel. It was quiet in the coach. Erica tip-toed to the bathroom and put her finger to her lips.

"Mia's asleep?" he whispered.

"Yes, and I don't want to wake her up," she said. "You want anything to eat from the fridge or the pantry? I'll bring it into the bedroom if you want."

"Any of those Greek yogurts left?" he whispered.

"Yeah," she said softly. "I'll grab what's left of the pita chips too, and a couple of water bottles."

"Perfect," Sam whispered. She snuck away. He finished drying off and slipped quickly into the bedroom.

"Well, I'm glad she fell asleep," Sam said. "That attack last night shattered her feeling of safety here. Hope she can get it back soon."

Erica nodded, taking off her robe and sitting on the bed in her nightgown. "I think she's gonna be fine. The times she's had with us aren't nearly as bad as the times she had before we got her."

"You're right about that. I'll never forget her face when she was tied up in that grocery store. Hope those experiences won't impact her life later on."

"She's got a lot of strength," Erica said. "Do you think we'll be able to stay here?"

"For the duration of the war? I doubt it."

"You think it'll be destroyed?"

He looked at the worry in her eyes. "No, but I don't think we can finish the fight from this location. We need to stop the enemy from opening that new route from Mexico. We screwed up this area for them already, with our destruction of the pass on Highway 94."

"Where will we have to be?"

"Look at the spots on the map where I-8 is close to the border, and the area around Calexico. Those are going to be battle zones. Same with the area near Yuma."

Erica picked up her phone and navigated the map program to those areas. "Okay, I see what you mean. You don't think they'll continue to hit us here just for revenge?"

"They're in enough trouble that they can't afford the luxury of revenge," Sam said. "I don't know this Daan Mertins, but I *do* know Saladin. He's a strategic thinker. He'll get pissed enough to throw a small number of men into a vendetta, but only if it won't hurt the larger mission. He figures if he can meet his goal of getting another six or seven hundred thousand enemy fighters over the border, he'll be able to take over this whole end of California, and be ready to attack the US Navy stronghold in San Diego."

"And if he knocks the US Navy out of San Diego, he can use the port to bring in even more Islamist fighters."

"Yeah," Sam said while he pulled the foil top off his yogurt. "Moving men in by ship is a whole lot easier than moving them through the desert."

"So how long do you think we'll stay here, then?"

"We need to watch the apps," Sam said. "Watch the area around Julian, for example. If they build up a lot of troops there, we'll get hit here."

"I thought you said he didn't care about revenge."

"If he can take us out, either by driving us north or killing us, he'll have a free hand to set up his supply routes. If he doesn't bring a bunch of his folks into Julian, it'll be because he wants to avoid fighting us until he has more men."

"You know where his men are now?" Erica asked.

"Spread out over hundreds of miles, but the furthest I've seen is Warner Springs."

"Crap, that's really close to Julian," Erica said.

"They've been there since this afternoon, sweetie. They might take Highway 78 east to Highway 86, which leads down to I-8 near El Centro. From there he could go east or west on I-8 to one of the two southern most spots, or go straight down to Calexico, as I just mentioned."

"What would you do?" Erica asked.

"Tough call, but I'd probably take Highway 78 east and avoid fighting us for now."

She grabbed the bag of pita chips and took out a few, then handed the bag to him. "I hope you're right. I'd rather chase him down someplace else than have him attack here."

Sam ate a few pita chips, then handed the bag back to her.

"Do you agree?" she asked.

"I want him to do whatever is most likely a mistake," Sam said. "To me, that would be gathering everybody up in Julian and trying to hit us."

"Dammit, I really don't want to be on the run again, especially with Mia."

"We might be able to fight them and win," Sam said.

"Not if they have two hundred thousand fighters."

Sam chuckled. "Ivan's recruitment team is focused on our area now, after pulling off a genius play up north. Twice. No, actually three times, although he wasn't solely responsible for the third."

"Not sure I get it."

"They recruited all those citizens for the battles in the Bay Area and Sacramento."

"What was the third one?"

"Portland," Sam said, "although there was a lot of local help in Oregon for that effort."

"Heard Karen and Dana talking about Portland. Still, two hundred thousand people? Could we really get that many?"

"Oregon is less populated than southern California, and they were able to get nearly two hundred thousand to join in the battles there."

"When will we know?" Erica asked.

"We'll just have to keep watching the apps. See if they continue south or head east. It's possible that they hang out for a while and do nothing, you know. Been watching the enemy troop movements in Mexico?"

"No, not much," Erica said. "What's going on?"

"About half of the original force has taken off, moving pretty quickly to the southeast. I think they're headed for Texas."

"That's good, isn't it?" Erica asked.

"For Texas, not so much. It *was* good for us."

"*Was?*"

"Yeah, Seth talked to us a few minutes before we left the Saloon."

"You didn't say anything to me?"

"Mia was with you the whole time, remember?"

"Oh, yeah," Erica said. "So?"

"Seth and Kaitlyn expanded the range of that history program. There's been new troops arriving at the port at Mazatlán. They appear to be heading north-west, towards the California border."

"How close are they?"

"Not very, but they're in a country where there's nobody to stop them. They'll be to the border in three or four days. I'm sure Saladin would like to lay out the welcome mat for them. It's more important for him than dealing with Dodge City."

She leaned back, laying her head on her pillow. "How am I supposed to sleep now?"

He looked into her eyes, rolling towards her, kissing her tenderly.

"Oh, God," she whispered.

"Think you can be quiet?" She nodded yes, her arms going around him.

4

Two Fronts

Ben Dover was in his social media control room, pacing, waiting for Ivan's call. His friends, many with him since his days at UC Santa Cruz, were watching him, worried. The phone rang. Ben leapt at it and hit the answer button on the speaker.

"Ivan?"

"Yes, Ben, sorry for the delay. Is there a problem?"

"We're not getting enough response in Eastern San Diego or Imperial counties."

"How many commitments so far?" Ivan asked.

"Just barely sixty thousand. It's not that the people aren't willing, it's just that the population is low, and there are a lot of retired folks who don't use the internet much. Word of mouth helps with that somewhat, but it takes time."

"I see," Ivan said. "I thought San Diego County had a large population."

"It's huge, but most of the people are in the area near the city, and the US Navy and Marines have that locked up pretty tight."

"You have a proposal, don't you?" Ivan asked.

"I want to expand our operation to LA, Orange, Riverside, and San Bernardino Counties," he said. "I think I can make a case that it's in their interest to join the battle."

"You want to tell them that if Saladin brings in more people through the southern border, they'll eventually be attacked," Ivan said, "and that's true. They're going to see it. Go ahead."

"You know there's a mix of folks in LA county, right? There are people there who prefer the stability of martial law. Crime is up there because the state government fell apart. Some parts of Orange, Riverside, and San Bernardino counties have a similar issue."

"Look at the Bay Area and Sacramento. You did well there."

"I know, Ivan, but that was right after the women told everyone about the UN Peacekeepers and their rape operation. It's been a while. People have short attention spans."

"What do you want from me?" Ivan asked. "There's something. I can tell by the tone of your voice."

"The optimum place to recruit is western San Diego County."

"Oh," Ivan said, silent for a moment. "I'll need to open a line of communications with the US Navy for that to work. They're avoiding direct contact with the resistance."

"I'm asking that you work that. Meanwhile I'll work those other counties."

"How many people do you think we need down there?" Ivan asked. "Saladin only has two hundred thousand on the way."

"Have you been watching Mazatlán?" Ben asked, shooting a glance at his friends, who were hanging on every word.

"Haven't been paying much attention since that's so far south. What are you seeing?"

"The enemy is pumping Islamists into that port like crazy," Ben said. "If it keeps up, we'll be back to the seven-hundred thousand level like we were before half of them headed southeast."

"You don't think our people down there can stop them, do you?"

"Two of my guys came from that area, and know the terrain. If the enemy lines up that many fighters along the border just about anywhere, they'll walk right in. Bottling up I-8 will stop them from moving trucks up north, but they can go through this area on foot like a frigging hurricane, take over, and then choose any road they like to go north."

Ivan was silent for more than a minute.

"You still there?" Ben asked.

"Yes, I'm thinking," Ivan said, silent again for a few minutes. Ben's team eyed him. You could hear a pin drop in the room.

"Okay, you've got me convinced that we have a problem," Ivan said. "I need to get on the horn with some folks. Start working everywhere except western San Diego county. I'll see if I can start up some dialog with the US Navy. Good enough?"

"Perfect, boss, thanks!" Ben said, smiling at his crew.

"Thanks for bringing this to my attention. You've got talents I didn't realize. Talk to you soon." The call ended. Ben's team cheered, rushing to him and patting him on the back.

***

Robbie woke up before the sun rose over the quarry lot, Morgan still snoring softly next to him. He snuck out of bed, dressed, and went to the dinette, sitting in front of his laptop, moving the mouse and waiting for the screen to wake up. When it did, he looked at the high-res app. His eyes got wide as he scrolled east on I-80.

"Dammit," he said, pulling his phone out and sending a text to the leadership. Then he switched on the coffee maker and went into the bedroom. "Morgan. We're about to have company. Better get dressed."

She rolled towards him, half asleep. "What?"

"The enemy is coming this way. I just sent a message to Jules and the others. They'll be here any minute."

"Oh," she said, sitting up quickly. "I'll get dressed. Did you turn on the coffee?"

"Yeah," he said, turning to leave. Somebody knocked on the door. "They're here." He rushed out to open it. Jules, Ted, and Sparky came in. Before they all got inside, Tex trotted over.

"Enemy move west on I-80?" Jules asked, leaning against the kitchen counter.

"You got it," Robbie said.

"How far, partner?" Tex asked.

"They're almost to Elko. That's about a third of the way."

"I was afraid of this," Sparky said.

"We need to hit them in the mountains," Ted said, "and we need help from the locals. There still two hundred thousand?"

"Less came across the border than that," Robbie said. "Looks like it's closer to a hundred and fifty thousand."

"What happened to the others?"

"Not sure," Robbie said. "They aren't on the road, so they're probably back in Salt Lake City."

"We have to leave now and attack," Ted said. "We'd better wake everybody up."

"Kid, start looking for good spot on I-80 where we can hit from side-roads," Jules said.

"Yeah, and see if you can find one where there's a bridge we could blow," Ted said. "So we can get them bottled up."

"I'll get on that right now," Robbie said.

"Okay, guys, let's get everybody going," Tex said. "We better leave in a half hour. No longer."

"I agree," Jules said. The men left the rig. Morgan came out of the bedroom.

"You hear that?" Robbie asked, eyes on his laptop screen.

"Yeah," she said. "Keep working. I'll get you a cup of coffee and a granola bar."

"Thanks," he said.

***

Clem was up early, looking out the window of his Dodge City Hotel room. The western street below was waking up. A horse-drawn wagon rolled by, carrying feed in the back, the driver seeing him and waving. His mind was on the surveillance task he'd be working later, when the others were up. There was a knock on the door. He answered it. Sarah stood before him.

"Oh, good, you're up," she said. "Heard you'd be going into town to get some electronics. Want some company for that?"

"Sure," he said. "Come on in."

She shot him a funny glance, and he laughed.

"What?"

"You looked nervous about being in my room. Sorry, Sarah, but that ship sailed quite a while ago. I just need to put my shoes on, and then we can get some breakfast. I smell coffee coming from downstairs."

"Oh," she said, looking embarrassed. "I didn't mean anything, really."

"I know. Just a sec." He sat on a chair by the bed and pulled on his walking shoes, lacing them slowly, his hands not moving as fast as they used to. "You staying here too?"

"I'm in the boarding house with Garrett's sister and a few others. She's a riot."

"Susanne. Fine woman. I'll bet she runs Garrett ragged."

"Well, Elmer at least," she said. "Her on again, off again boyfriend."

"I heard the on and off cycle is about every four hours."

Both chuckled as Clem stood. "My back is gonna be killing me tonight."

They went down the stairs. There was a continental breakfast laid out, with coffee in a large canister pot, and a sign saying *Help Yourselves.*

"Well isn't this nice?" Sarah asked.

"This breakfast is more John's style than mine," Clem said, wishing he could take it back when he saw the sadness in Sarah's eyes. "Sorry."

"Don't be silly," she said. "I do miss him so."

"Me too," Clem said. "Knew him for over forty years."

"I was married to him for thirty-five," she said. "I thought you were scary at first."

"Me? I'm a pussycat. Always have been."

"I know that now, but you were older, and a little stern."

He smiled as he drew himself a cup of coffee from the canister, taking a tentative sip. "It's pretty good."

They sat at one of the round tables near the wall. Elmer walked in, smiling when he saw the spread. "Good, I was hoping that'd be here."

"Where's Susanne?" Sarah asked. "Oh, and good morning."

"Good morning to you," he said as he got coffee. "Susanne's a working fool. She's down in the mine already, pushing the ammo loading team."

"You don't work with her on that operation?" Clem asked.

"Oh, *hell* no," he said. "You think I'd let her boss me around like that? I only allow that if it's in my interest." He shot Clem a wicked glance. Sarah cleared her throat.

"What's your job here?" Clem asked.

"Contractor," he said. "Built a lot of the town with a crew of folks. Helped them get up to code, too, after the first debacle."

"Oh, you didn't build the stuff that was torn down?" Clem asked.

He chuckled. "Nah, that was before I joined the group. They tried to build this place like a barn-raising. That's okay for a barn, but if you've got people living in it, the state cares very much about how the construction is done."

"I'd be surprised if the state would cut you slack on a barn anymore, actually," Clem said.

Elmer stuffed the last of a Danish into his mouth, chewing it quick so he could respond.

"Take your time," Clem said, catching a smirk from Sarah.

"Sorry," Elmer said. "Kinda looks like I was raised in a barn, I reckon."

They all laughed.

"But you're right," Elmer continued. "The damn state has rules for anything you build now. Even the stuff that really don't matter. Sick to death of it, but I know how to work the system to get things done. They hired me to help, and I kinda fell in love with the place."

Susanne came stomping into the lobby. "Where's that old goat Willard?"

"What's the matter, honey bun?" Elmer asked.

"That's for the guests," she said, eyeing the Danish in his hand.

Elmer smiled at her and took a bite. She growled at him.

"What do you want Willard for?" he asked.

"Those damn lights that he strung up in the mine shaft quit working," she said. "I need them on. We've got a quota to make."

"Okay, I'll grab Willard and drag him down there. He needs to know how to do that right. I'll show him, okay?"

She looked at him for a second. "Why was he doing it instead of you, anyway?"

"I was busy working something for Garrett, remember?"

She thought for a moment. "Oh, hell, I don't remember what you're talking about. No matter. Grab him and get down there pronto. Oh, and if you find more booze down there, tell me about it this time." She left in a huff.

"She's always going full speed, isn't she?" Clem asked.

"Brother, you don't know the half of it." Elmer washed down the second Danish with coffee and left, tipping his hat.

"Wow," Sarah said, shaking her head.

"I kinda like it here," he said. "Call me crazy. Wonder how you become a permanent resident?"

"Are you serious?"

"It's not like we can go back to the RV Park in Dulzura," he said, sadness in his eyes. "I miss Harry and Nancy."

"And Connie and Hank too," Sarah said, eyes tearing up. "And my John."

"Let's change the subject or I'll be blubbering like an old fool."

"You aren't an old fool," she said.

Sid came in with Yvonne. "Oh, there you guys are. Meeting in five minutes."

"With who?"

"Ji-Ho is calling it, and they're setting up the audio-visual stuff. I think they might need your help, Clem."

"Okay, done with breakfast anyway," he said. "Where?"

"Saloon," Sid said.

"Good, about time for a beer."

"Now you're talking," Sid said, both women rolling their eyes. They all left, walking down the wooden sidewalk to the saloon, which was already full with people arriving for the meeting.

"Somebody open windows," Ji-Ho said, "so overflow crowd can listen." He was up front next to the TV. "Oh, Clem, good, come help please."

Clem nodded, making his way through the crowd.

"Hi, Auntie Sarah," Mia said, rushing over to her.

"Well hi yourself, sweetie," Sarah said, stroking her hair as she watched people coming in.

"Is this gonna be scary?"

"If it is, I can take you for a walk to see the horses," Sarah said.

"That would be fun," Mia said.

"She's not bothering you, I hope?" Erica asked, walking up with Sam.

"No, of course not. I told her if the discussion got too scary I'd take her to see the horses."

"You don't have to do that," Erica said.

"I wouldn't mind a bit."

"Wish this place was bigger," Sam said.

"It'll be good enough," Garrett said, coming from the back of the saloon with Anna and Willard. "I'll make sure all my men get the word. Most of them are out on patrol, and that's where we need them."

"It ready," Ji-Ho said. "I'll send text to Ivan."

People found places to sit, lean, or just stand as the TV came on, Clem coming out from behind the screen with a laptop on a long HDMI cable. He set it on a bar stool facing the crowd, open so the camera could pick up at least half of the people in the saloon.

Ivan walked onto the frame, wearing his pin-striped suit and fedora, sitting to face the camera. "Hello, all. Can you hear me?"

"Yep," Clem said. "Should I patch in Ben Dover now?"

"Yes, please," Ivan said. Clem typed on the laptop, moving his finger on the touch pad a couple times, and then the screen split into two, with Ben Dover on the right pane and Ivan on the left. Ben's hair looked like he just got up, and he was wearing a t-shirt with a stretched neck.

"You hear me?" Ben asked.

"We do," Ji-Ho said.

"Yep, I can hear both of you," Ivan said.

Ji-Ho smiled. "Okay, we set. Go ahead."

"Hello, all, thanks for your attention," Ivan said. "Ben has been working recruitment for your area. In the process, him and his team came to some conclusions, and they convinced me to act on what they were telling me. Ben, please tell the team what you see."

"Have any of you seen the buildup of enemy forces through the port at Mazatlán?" Ben asked.

"I have," Seth said. "It's got me worried."

"It should," Ben said. "Last time I checked, they were up to about five hundred thousand fighters."

"There's more off-shore," Seth said. "Another two hundred thousand at least."

A gasp went up in the room.

"We can't take on that many fighters," Susanne said. "I'm having a hard time keeping ammo production high enough for the current scale of battle."

"So we have to stop up I-8 and the other routes across the border," Angel said.

"That won't be enough," Ed said, his face grave. "With those kinds of numbers, they can march over the border on foot, kill everybody around, and choose the northbound route they want to take."

"He's exactly right," Ben said. "We'll have to recruit our way out of this, and we'll need coordination when the volunteers arrive, plus a place for them to stay until the battle, and a method for them to get *to* the battle."

"How can we recruit that many people?" Kaitlyn asked.

"We have to recruit from all the counties in Southern California," Ivan said. "Especially LA and Orange counties. That's where the numbers are."

"What about western San Diego county?" Sam asked. "That's not as large as LA county, but it's larger than Orange county and closer, too."

"We're trying to contact the US Navy to make that happen," Ivan said. "It's difficult."

"I know some people," Sam said. "I can work that with you."

"That would be very much appreciated," Ivan said.

"What are we gonna do?" Trevor asked. "How can we help?"

"Here's my proposal," Ivan said. "We go after all the recruitment we can, including western San Diego county if we can get agreement with the US Navy. We use your Dodge City as a staging area. Is it large enough for the number of people we're talking about?"

"And then some, if you're just talking land," Garrett said. "Food and shelter will be something else again."

"We'll work that," Ivan said. "Tents and food as well as military weapons to arm people, so they don't have to go against such a huge force with hunting rifles."

"I pledge whatever help we can provide," Garrett said. "Anybody object?"

"Hell no," Willard shouted.

"I'm for it of course," Elmer said.

"Me too," shouted somebody else.

"What about more battle wagon and off-roader?" Ji-Ho asked. "Still come?"

"Those have been on the way for a couple days," Ivan said. "They'll be there soon. We also sent military small arms and ammo—enough to outfit a force of a thousand men. We'll obviously have to expand this quite a bit for the new recruits."

"Where are you getting all this stuff?" Trevor asked. "Never mind, I don't want to know."

Ivan chuckled. "Some of the weapons will be AK-47s and other European weapons, by the way. When we kicked those cretins out of the Bay Area and Sacramento, we captured a lot of military hardware."

"No problem here," Sam said. "AKs jam less often than M16s."

"You have more to say, Ben?" Ivan asked.

"Yeah," Ben said. "Don't destroy roads down there. You'll need them to access the enemy."

"Roger that," Sid said.

"Okay, anything else before I go work this?" Ivan asked.

"Good luck, and let us know if you need help from us," Sam said.

"Yes, we at your service," Ji-Ho said.

Ivan smiled. "I know, guys. It's an honor to serve with you. Talk to you soon." With that he and Ben Dover left the screen.

"Wow," Seth said to Trevor. "This is gonna be insane."

"Seriously, dude," Trevor said, Angel nodding in agreement.

Clem finished unhooking the audio-visual stuff. Sarah walked over. "You still doing the surveillance task today?"

"Yep," he said. "More important than ever, in my estimation. This is about to become ground central for the California Resistance."

"I think we'd better nix that idea of putting land mines out," Sid said. Yvonne laughed. "You got that right, brother," Clem said.

{5}

Towle Bridges

Morgan was driving the battle wagon, climbing into the Sierra foothills on I-80, the generator purring softly to keep a good charge on Robbie's laptop. They'd been on the road for just over an hour. Robbie was sitting in the passenger seat, computer on his lap.

"Bingo!" he said. "I think I finally found a good place."

"How far?" Morgan asked.

"Twenty minutes, assuming we can keep this speed. Towle, Alta and Baxter."

"That's three places," she said.

"We'll need to blow a bridge at Towle, and have a couple battle wagons at an off-ramp at Crystal Springs Road, and another couple at Baxter road."

"Oh," she said, glancing at him for a moment. "Sounds complicated."

"I wish we had another three or four battle wagons, but in this situation the off-roaders might be better anyway. I need to get Jules on the phone. You can shut down the generator now. This thing has enough charge for the rest of the operation."

"Okay," Morgan said, reaching to shut it off. Robbie pulled out his cellphone and hit Jules's contact, then put it on speaker.

"Robbie, what got for me?" Jules asked. "Sparky in coach too."

"Hey, Robbie," Sparky said.

"Hi, guys. I found a good place, but it's gonna require that we handle three locations."

"Uh oh," Sparky said.

"No, I expect," Jules said. "Where, kid?"

"We blow a bridge at Towle. It's in a place they can't get around, unless they're before the off-ramps at Crystal Springs Road or Baxter Road."

"I get," Jules said. "This be long caravan. We stop detour. I like."

"Doesn't that cut us a little thin?" Sparky asked. "We only have six battle wagons."

"We've got all the off-roaders," Robbie said. "In this terrain, they're probably better than having a bunch more battle wagons. We can roll down the side roads, blasting all their vehicles with the M19s from behind a fair amount of cover."

"Yes," Jules said. "How long?"

"We'll be there in about twenty minutes," Robbie said.

"Pretty good plan, Robbie," Sparky said. "Those three locations stretch out a little under two miles, according to my GPS app. It's doable."

"What about this off-ramp at Kearsarge Mill Road?" Dana asked.

"Look at where that leads," Robbie said. "If you get off there, the alternate from the right side of I-80 just dumps you back onto westbound I-80 or back towards the east, and if you go under the interstate and try to take the roads on the left side, they all dead-end except one."

"What about the one?" Jules asked.

Sparky laughed. "I see what he's saying. That route leads you over some pretty dicey roads for big vehicles, and when it dumps back to I-80, they'll be blocked by the fallen bridge at Towle. Genius, kid."

"Okay, relay info to the rest of team," Jules said. "We'll notify demolition team. We blow bridge as soon as we get to Towle. Where enemy?"

"Just about to Imlay, Nevada," Dana said.

"When do they get to Towle?" Jules asked.

"Over three hours," Dana said. "We'll have two and a half hours to blow the bridge and get set up at the other off-ramps. It'll be tight, but not too tight."

"Perfect," Jules said. "Thanks, Robbie. We spread word."

The call ended. Morgan looked over at him. "Nice job, honey."

"Thanks," Robbie said. "Hope nothing goes wrong."

They drove the next fifteen minutes with very little conversation, Robbie watching the high-res app. The enemy continued their relentless drive west, but their speed didn't increase.

"You're getting nervous," Morgan said, glancing at him.

"Just trying to broaden my thinking," he said. "The enemy force is still stretched out a long way."

"You're worried that when the first group gets to the ruined bridge in Towle, there will be forces far enough back to turn around before they get stuck."

"Exactly," he said. "We have geography in our favor, though. There's a place they can turn around before Kearsarge Mill Road. It's called Whitmore Road, but they can't continue west from there. All they can do is switch over to the eastbound I-80."

"How far back is that?"

Robbie looked at his computer screen for a moment. "About six miles."

"And how far spread out are the enemy right now?"

"More like ten miles," Robbie said. "It's better than it was, though. Before it was about fifty miles, so they are tightening up."

"Maybe we should send another team east to bottle up Whitmore Road, then," Morgan said. "To keep them from escaping. Doesn't have to be something permanent. Just enough to hold them there while we destroy them."

"I don't know if we have enough ammo to do that. If they're all stopped, we'll have a couple hundred troops getting out of vehicles and shooting at our off-roaders."

"Oh," she said. "So we should just do what we can, and then get our people out of harm's way?"

"That's what I'm thinking. If we can nail a good part of their forces and stop them from using I-80, their job becomes much more difficult."

"We're almost there," Morgan said. "You gonna bring this up with Jules?"

"Yeah," Robbie said. "Get off at Morton Road, and we'll take Casa Loma Road to the bridge."

"Will do. What if half their force turns around and goes east on I-80. Is there another way they could come west?"

"I'm looking," Robbie said, eyes glued to his screen. He chuckled. "No, they're really screwed, since we control most of Northern California now. They could get on Highway 395 from Reno and go way north, then cross over to I-5 and head into Sacramento that way, but I don't see them doing it."

"Why not?"

"It's way out of the way, and they'll need to get fuel for their convoy in areas that we control. We'll blow them away."

Robbie's phone rang. "Jules," he said, hitting the speaker button.

"Hey, Robbie, don't take off-ramp. Pull to side of I-80 before bridge. We fire at enemy from there."

"Oh, okay," Robbie said. "Glad you got us. We were about to get off onto Casa Loma."

"Dead ends, too low to fire at enemy on I-80."

"Okay," Robbie said. "I assume most of the battle wagons and off-roaders are going on. How are they getting home?"

"Dana work out. Baxter Road to Alta Bonnynook Road," Jules said. "Long out of way. We be home before them, if plans go well."

"What's to keep the enemy from following that way?" Morgan asked.

"We ruin their vehicles on off-ramps at Crystal Springs and Baxter, plus stop up I-80 with broken trucks too. They eventually get through, but take long time, after many killed. I think they turn tail and go east instead."

"We're coming up to it already," Morgan said, pulling to the side of the road.

"Do K-turn and back up to bridge," Jules said. "We high-tail west when done, get onto westbound side when can. Got? Talk to you soon."

"Yeah, we got it," Robbie said. The call ended. Morgan looked in her mirror. "Good thing there's no traffic on this road. She turned on the wide highway, pulled over to the right shoulder, and backed up.

"Here comes Jules," Robbie said, watching him make the turn and back up on the left shoulder.

"We should angle these," Morgan said, looking out the window. "Otherwise the mini-gun turret will block the grenade launcher turret."

Robbie looked outside and nodded in agreement. "Do that. I'll text Jules."

He sent the text as Morgan adjusted the position of their coach, and then they both got outside. Jules angled his coach and joined them.

"Good point, kid," Jules said.

"That was Morgan's idea," Robbie said.

"Really? Very impressive."

"Thanks," Morgan said. Shelly, Dana, and Sparky came out.

"We'd better get to one side or another so the rest of our rigs can get through," Sparky said.

Jules nodded, and all of them came to the right shoulder next to Robbie and Morgan's coach.

"Who's going where?" Robbie asked.

"We stay here," Jules said. "You too. Please keep eye on the laptop and let us know status as operation runs."

"Will do," Robbie said.

"Tex and Cody stay at Crystal Springs Road. Ted and Justin go on to Baxter Road. We distribute off-roaders between the three areas and on the roads in-between and past Baxter."

"Here comes more of our folks," Sparky said, pointing as two of the battle wagons and several dozen off-roaders raced by. Six off-roaders pulled up next to them.

"We ready to blow the bridges?" asked one of the men after lifting the face screen on his helmet. "We've got the explosives and stuff in our saddle bags."

"Yes, do, westbound side first please," Jules said.

"You heard the man," the off-roader said. "Let's go back to Casa Loma road."

"Maybe we should blast this guard rail with a grenade or two," said a second man. "We could get down there with ease. It's not even steep."

"No," Jules said. "Save grenades for enemy. We have lots coming."

"Roger that," the lead man said. They turned their off-roaders and raced back, staying to the shoulder as more off-roaders and the last two battle wagons raced by in the left lane.

"Sure those guys know what they're doing?" Sparky asked.

Jules smiled. "Yes, did jobs for Ivan before. Top notch."

"Do we even need to blow the eastbound bridge?" Robbie asked. "That center divider is pretty tough."

"Yes, do," Jules said. "They be in panic to get to other side. Ram with vehicles to knock over, or use explosives. We need both sides down."

"Yeah, I agree," Sparky said.

"I go," Jules said, "and get into siege mode. You should do same."

Robbie nodded, and climbed into the coach behind Morgan, who went to the driver's side and flipped the switch for siege mode.

"Should I raise the guns now?" she asked.

"Wait," Robbie said, as he pulled out the machine gun tray in front of the passenger side. "Let's see if we're angled so we can hit the westbound side of the road with the rear guns."

"Good idea," she said, watching as he looked through the target reticle.

"It's about perfect where it is. We can hit the westbound and eastbound sides with it right now." He pulled out his phone and sent a text to Jules, then picked up his laptop and opened the high-res app. Morgan set up siege mode and raised the weapons.

Robbie's phone dinged. "Jules is doing the same thing."

"Yeah, I see him jockeying around," Morgan said, looking through the main sight. "Wonder if the enemy will drive all the way up here or stop dead in their tracks when they see our rigs?"

"Good question," Robbie said. "Maybe we ought to be hidden instead of sticking out like a sore thumb over here."

"We'd have to go down a ways to be out of sight, wouldn't we?"

Robbie looked at his map program, zooming out. "There's a nice curve not very far back there. Maybe we ought to go past it, and wait for a tip-off from the off-roaders." He typed the message to Jules, who called after a moment.

"Robbie, that good idea," Jules said. "Let's come out of siege mode and do that. See how many enemy vehicles fly off end of road. I tell other coaches to get out of sight too. We pack them in tight."

"Excellent," Robbie said. "See you around the bend."

Jules chuckled and ended the call.

"Okay, take us back out of siege mode," Robbie said.

"Good." Morgan flipped the switches to get them back into travel mode and they drove forward, Robbie watching through the sight. They went around the bend and up another fifty yards, Jules catching up with them after a couple minutes.

"Okay, this ought to do it," Robbie said. He looked at the laptop again.

"Where are they?" Morgan asked.

"The first of them are getting into Sparks. It's just east of Reno."

"Wow, they're making good time," she said. "Oh crap."

"What?" Robbie asked, looking up, seeing two CHP cruisers roll up next to Jules's coach. "Uh oh."

Two officers got out of each cruiser, walking up to meet Jules, who was walking towards them. They shook hands warmly. Robbie chuckled.

"I'll bet he called them in to put a roadblock out here," Morgan said.

"That's what I'm thinking. We made some good friends at their headquarters after we helped them beat the enemy."

The officers got into their vehicles, rolled back to where the last off-ramp was, and set up a roadblock. Jules sent a text, which Robbie read.

"Now we won't have unwelcome guests," the text read. Robbie sent a quick reply and then went back to his laptop.

"I was a little worried about that," Robbie said. "Kept forgetting to bring it up."

"Yeah, I know, me too. I guess we just wait now."

There was a loud blast, vibrating the road beneath them, then another. They could hear chunks of cement falling. Robbie raced out the door and looked to the east. A grey cloud of dust was rising, and a few whoops and hollers could be heard.

"Wow," Morgan said, coming up behind him to look. "That made a good rumble."

Jules came out of his rig with a big grin on his face, followed by Shelly and Dana. "Nice show, no?"

"Damn straight, man," Robbie shouted back.

"Where enemy?"

"Just east of Reno and coming fast," Robbie said.

"Fire in the hole!" somebody yelled to the east, and there were two more massive explosions, raising more dust, the road under their feet vibrating.

"We should've waited for a few minutes before we moved," Shelly said. Dana looked at her and laughed as Sparky came out to join them.

"I'm gonna go inside and get back on the laptop," Robbie shouted. He and Morgan climbed into their coach.

"Well?" Morgan asked as he looked at the screen.

"They're just past Reno now. Looks like they stretched out more, though. Some of them slowed down."

"Maybe that's bad," Morgan said. "How far back are the last of them?"

He looked at the screen, then smiled. "Lockwood. They're still only ten miles from start to finish. We're gonna get most of them."

***

Clem, Sarah, Sid, and Yvonne were coming home from Dulzura, after shopping all morning for electronic surveillance gear, food, and clothing.

"I'm surprised they had so much good surveillance stuff," Clem said. "Should just open a tab with that place."

Sid snickered. "What kind of guy names his electronics store *Scooter's*?"

"Really," Yvonne said. "Sounds like the name of a bar, not a geek store."

"Hey, watch that," Clem said. They all cracked up.

"Want to stop anywhere else?" Sid asked.

"We're burning daylight," Clem said. "We probably should spend the rest of the day getting the cameras set up by that fence break."

"No rest for the weary," Sid said.

Clem shot him a glance. "I can handle it if you're tired."

"I'm joking," Sid said, "and I'm not letting you go out there by yourself. Hell, I'm not letting anybody go out there by themselves. Remember what happened to Ed?"

"Ed," Clem said. "Maybe we should see if he wants to take us in his hovercraft. Probably make better time."

"Is it fixed?" Sarah asked. "Haven't heard it for a while."

"As far as I know," Sid said. "We need to bring some heavier tools. I think the Jeep might be better."

Clem smiled. "Probably right." They made the turn onto Campbell Ranch road.

"Almost home," Sid said. "Another ten miles to town."

"Yeah, well don't go too fast," Yvonne said. "I heard somebody almost hit a cow the other day on this road."

"You seem awful nervous, honey." Sid glanced at her for a moment as the Jeep bounced along.

"We have seven hundred thousand bad guys on their way across the border," Yvonne said, "and another couple hundred thousand on their way down from northern California. This is the makings of a clusterfuc…"

"Stop!" Sarah said quickly, putting her hand over her mouth. "Sorry."

Sid and Yvonne laughed, Clem showing a sheepish grin.

"I guess I don't need to use crude language all the time," Yvonne said. "Sorry."

"Oh, it's just me," Sarah said. "I used to do that to John. Surprised he put up with it all those years."

They rode quietly for a while, seeing a couple of vehicles racing to the highway, and a few cows off to the right side of the road, pausing from their grazing to watch them go by.

"You really want to see if you can stay here, Clem?" Sarah asked.

"Here?" Yvonne asked. "Please."

"I like it," Clem said. "Nice folks, cool surroundings, lots to do. I could get used to it."

"Where do you want to go after this is over?" Sarah asked Yvonne.

"Don't know," she said. "I don't think I can go back to the Dulzura RV Park."

"Me neither," Sid said. "Maybe a reservation? Either my tribe or yours?"

"That'll take some thought," Yvonne said. "I left for a reason."

Sid sighed. "I know, so did I. Maybe it's time to get lost in an urban area again. Been a while."

"We're not going back to Hawaiian Gardens," Yvonne said. "It's got to be someplace nicer than that."

"What?" Sid asked.

"How about Newport?" Clem quipped, which got a hearty laugh from Sid.

"Hell, like they'd let us in there."

"If we had the money, I'm sure they would," Yvonne said, "and therein lies the problem."

Everyone's phone dinged with a broadcast text.

"Uh oh," Yvonne said, pulling her phone out of the glovebox. "Meeting again."

"Saloon, I hope?" Sid asked. Yvonne elbowed him. "Hey, I'm driving here."

"Yep, it is the Saloon," Clem said. "Goody. I could use a beer. It's not too early this time."

"I think I know what this is about," Sid said, looking at his rear-view mirror. "Look back there."

They all looked, seeing a new battle wagon on the road about a hundred yards behind them, followed by two semi-trucks and a long line of additional battle wagons behind.

"Geez," Clem said. "Where's all this money coming from?"

"Ivan and Ji-Ho are both quite wealthy, apparently," Sarah said, "but I'll bet there are lots of interested parties who want to help this cause."

"You got that right," Sid said. "Here comes Sam's Jeep and a couple of Ji-Ho's. They're probably coming to meet them." He slowed to a stop as the oncoming Jeeps did, Sid getting his window next to Sam's.

"Get what you needed in town?" Sam asked. Mia waved to him from the back seat.

"Hi, darlin," Sid said, waving back to Mia, then looking at Sam. "Yeah, there's a great electronics joint there. Is the meeting about the delivery?" He nodded behind him.

"I wish," Sam said. Erica looked over from the passenger seat, fear in her eyes.

"Oh, crap, what now?" Clem asked.

"Good news and bad news," Sam said. "On the good side, the Islamists coming from the north *did* go east. They're trying to avoid us."

"What's the bad news?"

"Five hundred thousand Islamists are massing south of the border, and we don't have enough people there to stop them."

"Oh, God," Yvonne said. "This is what I was afraid of."

"It might not be too bad," Sam said. "Ivan contacted the US Armed forces in San Diego. Both the Navy and the Marines. There's no agreement on them getting directly involved yet, but we *have* been allowed to recruit citizens in western San Diego County. That might be enough."

"We'd better go, honey, so the caravan doesn't get held up too much," Erica said. "That meeting is soon. We need to be involved."

"Got it," Sam said. "See you guys in town."

He drove off, and Sid started moving again.

"Well, this could be worse," Clem said. Sarah glanced at him, then out the window as the Jeep got back to full speed.

6

Jacumba Hot Springs

Doug Westin looked at the border fence from his trench, right behind Old Highway 80, west of Jacumba Hot Springs. It looked like a tall picket fence–vertical metal bars with sheet metal on the top quarter, making it harder to climb. He raised the binoculars to his eyes and stared, panning from west to east. He was a large middle-aged man with graying hair receding from his forehead, and a goatee. Another man approached, a younger Hispanic with a medium build and jet-black hair, clean shaven. Doug looked over at him and smiled.

"Jorge, there you are," Doug said.

"See anything?" He got down into the trench next to Doug and lifted his own binoculars, scanning the area.

"Nope," Doug said. "Wish we had those apps. It would help. We could have a thousand enemy fighters right south of those hills."

"Do those apps really exist?"

"People I trust said so," Doug said. "That damn fence isn't going to slow anybody down for long."

Jorge chuckled. "At least we can see through it, man. Even if we had the big wall you wanted, they'd just blast through it, and we wouldn't be able to see as well as we can now."

Doug grinned. "Funny how this worked out. We fought like cats and dogs over the border wall. Now look at us. Comrades in arms."

"Keeping my people out is one thing," Jorge said. "Keeping out enemy Islamists is something very different."

"True, my friend," Doug said. "We get any more volunteers? I heard there's been a bunch of recruitment happening on the internet."

"Yeah, my kid brother said we have gobs of people coming from all over,"

"Hope they get here soon," Doug said. "Our three hundred men won't last long."

"True that," Jorge said. His phone dinged. He pulled it from his pocket and looked, eyes getting wide.

"What?"

"My kid brother Luis," he said. "There's twenty thousand citizens in Jacumba right now, armed to the teeth. A lot of them have military weapons."

"Thank God," Doug said. "We just might live through this. Where are they coming from?"

"Wow. All over… as far north as LA County. He said they were recruited by Ivan the Butcher."

"It's about time that guy noticed we've got a problem on the border," Doug said. "Are they coming here?"

"Yep, they want to be in the spots where the border is closest to a road, and this stretch is one of the best."

"When will they be here?" Doug asked.

"Any minute," Jorge said, sending a reply. After a few seconds, his phone dinged. "Oh, God."

"What?"

"Some of those guys have these apps, and they showed Luis. There's half a million Islamists about sixty-five miles from the border."

Doug's forehead broke out in a sweat. "Say again?"

"You heard me, man," Jorge said.

"We're dead. Maybe we should take off, and live to fight another day."

"Look, here comes a big line of vehicles," Jorge said. "Let's go meet them."

They climbed out of their trench, rushing to the road. The lead vehicle was a commercial bus. Doug and Jorge rushed towards the door just as it opened. A large middle-aged man in camo came down the steps, his hawkish eyes scanning the area, then walking towards them. He set down the weapons he carried–an M4 and an M60.

"You Doug and Jorge?" the man asked.

"Yep," Jorge said. "You talked to Luis?"

"Yeah," he said, shaking hands with them. "I'm head of the resistance in San Bernardino. Conrad Kowalski."

"You were recruited by Ivan the Butcher?" Doug asked.

"His recruitment leader, Ben Dover," he said, a smirk on his face.

"Oh yeah, that guy," Doug said. "Saw that video of him on the TV show. Love to shake his hand."

"Me too," Jorge said. "There really half a million enemy fighters down south?"

"Hey, Conrad, where do you want us?" shouted a man from the second vehicle–a stake truck with men jumping out of the bed. He was much younger, with the look of an army recruit.

"Let's move the vehicles off the road, and bring up the K-rail tenders. Place the K-rails about five feet apart, all up and down the road as far as we can. Got it?"

"You don't want them flush, so there's no gaps?"

"We don't have enough," Conrad said. "Stake them down, too, but place them first, okay?"

"Yeah, okay," the man said. "I'll pass the word."

Conrad waved the man off, then pulled his cellphone out, fired up the long-range app, and showed it to Jorge and Doug. "See all these icons here?"

"Yeah," Jorge said. "Holy crap."

"That's one way to say it," Conrad said, smiling. "*I'd* use a little stronger language."

"How'd you get this?" Doug asked.

"Go on the recruiting site and sign up, and you can download it. Worth it. What's your email addresses?"

They both told Conrad what they were, and he sent them emails with the link to the recruitment page.

"Thanks, man," Jorge said.

"How many people we got coming?" Doug asked.

"Not enough yet," Conrad said. "I know of eighty-thousand on the way, but they might not make it here in time. Obviously that's not enough. The only way we'll survive is to get a whole lot of recruits from San Diego. Ben Dover started recruiting there last night, and I hear the response is huge."

"Good," Doug said. "Ah, the app finished loading."

"Mine too," Jorge said. "I'm gonna forward this link to everybody on our team."

"Yeah, you do that," Doug said. "I've got the long-range app up now. There's gonna be more than half a million. I see a long trail of icons stretching up from the south."

"Yep, I've heard it could be as many as seven hundred thousand," Conrad said. "Take a look to the north-east."

"In Mexico?"

Conrad smiled. "I wish. California."

Doug moved his fingers around, his brow furrowed. "Highway 78, almost to Salton Sea. How many is that?"

"They're pretty stretched out, but I've heard about two-hundred thousand."

"Hell, man, they've got almost a million men on the way," Jorge said. "We can't counter that."

"There's ten million people in LA County. Over three million in San Diego County, and almost that many in Orange County. Riverside and San Bernardino each have over two million. We can field over a million citizens, easy. Look at what was done in Texas, and Northern California, and Portland."

"But in what amount of time?" Jorge asked.

"Well, I won't kid you guys. We might be overrun and killed before this starts rolling, but these heathens aren't going to win the war. No way, no how. We've already taken back Northern California, you know, and we own LA and Orange Counties."

"Where the hell are the Marines?" Doug asked. "Camp Pendleton is nearby."

"Maybe they're in with the Feds," Jorge said.

"They're not," Conrad said. "I've heard they're being used to make sure the Navy base doesn't get overrun. I agree that they ought to be helping us down here. It's in their interest, after all."

"Some Navy planes could be helpful too," Doug said. "There aren't enough Marines here to hold off a force the size that we're seeing."

Cars were leaving the road now, backing up and heading for the large flat areas between their position and Jacumba. Then two huge tenders rolled past them, and crews used the built-on cranes to lift K-rails onto the right shoulder of the highway.

"This is gonna take too long," Doug said.

Jorge chuckled. "See where the enemy is right now? There's no roads there. These folks are on foot. It takes a long time to march sixty-five miles on foot, man."

"Yep, that's why we're taking the time to do this," Conrad said. "Here's a good rule of thumb. Infantry can march about twenty-five miles per day. We've got two and a half days before the main enemy force gets here. Oh, and by the way, our recruits can drive here. It's all about the recruiting at this point."

Jorge's phone dinged again. He looked at it. "Luis. Another twenty-thousand citizens just got to town." He laughed. "The traffic is a frigging mess. Maybe we'll be okay after all."

"We'd better have them park there and walk here," Conrad said. "You know the right people to call about that?"

"Yeah," Doug said, pulling out his phone.

"I got to go check on some stuff," Conrad said. "Nice to meet you guys. I'm sure we'll see each other a lot in the next few days."

Jorge and Doug watched as he walked away with several of his men.

***

The battle wagons were all in place on I-80.

"This waiting is driving me nuts," Shelly said. She was sitting at the dinette in their battle wagon, watching the high-res app on her laptop. "Hey, honey, we'd better run the generator for a while so I can charge this up."

"No problem," Jules said. He flipped the switch on the dash to start it. "How close are they?"

"The lead is right by Lake Putt," she said. "The tail is just past Emigrant Gap."

"How far apart are those two places?" Sparky asked.

"Just a sec," Shelly said, typing on her laptop. "They've tightened up nicely. It's only four and a half miles."

"Perfect," Sparky said. "The entire group will be in the kill zone before the first of them hit the busted bridge."

"Yes, this almost too good to be true," Jules said.

"That's what worries me," Dana said. "We've got a multitude of enemy fighters coming at a small number of folks."

"We not stand and fight all," Jules said. "Never plan that. Stop them from coming to Sacramento. Kill a bunch, then get away clean. That's objective."

"I agree, but I share Dana's concern," Sparky said. "As soon as the first vehicles go over the edge, you know messages are gonna be sent to the vehicles behind them, right?"

"We can attack the back end as soon as this starts," Shelly said. "If we disable enough vehicles back there, it'll be hard for them to escape."

"That job of off-roaders by Baxter," Jules said. "Placed more there than at Crystal Springs road."

"I think they're speeding up," Shelly said. "The leaders just passed Whitmore Road."

"Won't be long now," Sparky said.

"We still gonna back up there?" Dana asked.

"Probably best way, so we can leave fast," Sparky said. "How do you feel about driving there backwards, Jules?"

"Piece of cake," he said. "New back end armor keep us safe until we get into siege mode."

"We shouldn't go right to the edge," Shelly said. "We've got the range to hit them from a further distance."

"True," Jules said. "Off-roaders do a lot more damage. Send text to Robbie. Only go far enough to see enemy, not all the way to edge."

"We're doing too much on-the-fly in this operation," Sparky said. "Ought to be by the numbers."

"We by numbers where need," Jules said. "We aren't important group, now that bridges down. Baxter group important, and strategy worked out well there."

"That's where Ted is, right?" Sparky asked, a sly smile coming on his face. "Say no more."

"Yes, he handle," Jules said. "He *always* handle."

***

Ted and Bryan sat at the dinette opposite Haley and Brianna.

"Where are the off-roaders now?" Ted asked.

Brianna pulled out her phone and clicked the Find My Friends app, watching it for about thirty seconds. "Still on the eastbound side of I-80," she said.

"Well they'd better get to Kearsarge Mill Road in the next five minutes, or they'd better get off into the woods on the side of the road," Haley said, watching the high-res app on her laptop. "The lead group of enemy vehicles is pretty damn close to there now."

"There's guard rail all along there," Bryan said, "until they get to the off-ramp for Drum Forebay, and they'd better turn right and go down a ways, or they'll be seen."

"How do you know that?" Brianna asked.

"The map program," Bryan said. "Street view."

"Oh," she said, "that's smart."

"Says the woman who came up with using Find my Friends to track our off-roaders," Ted said, smiling at her. "So impressed. You made my job much easier."

"Seriously," Haley said.

"We all used that, before the war," Brianna said, her babyface turning red. Bryan looked at her, the affection showing to everybody.

"This is gonna be close," Haley said, refreshing her screen to see the new position of the enemy. "They're three miles from Kearsarge right now."

"And the off-roaders are a mile and a half, but they're slower," Brianna said. "Not that much slower, though."

"Thank God for that," Haley said. "This makes me nervous as hell."

"Tell me about it," Brianna said.

"Dammit, I wish we'd get past this part," Bryan said. "They there yet?"

Brianna looked at her phone again. "They can probably see the sign for the off-ramp right now."

"Enemy's less than a mile away," Haley said. "Geez."

"We're gonna make it," Ted said. "There's no traffic light at the top of that off-ramp, is there?"

"Stop sign," Bryan said. "No traffic, either, so they'll be able to get around that corner in a hurry."

"The first of them made it up the ramp!" Brianna said.

"You can't tell where the end is, can you?" Haley asked.

"Nope. Should've talked to whoever was going to be last."

"How close are the enemy fighters?" Ted asked.

"Less than half a mile," Haley said.

"Arrrggg," Bryan said. "C'mon, guys, make it!"

"Quarter mile," Haley said.

Brianna's phone dinged. "They're all past the right turn."

"Yes!" Bryan said, leaning back in his seat, taking a deep breath.

Haley smiled. "And there go the bad guys, racing past it."

"So now we wait," Ted said. "Is the enemy convoy still looking like about five miles long?"

"Four and a half," Haley said. "How can this be going so well?"

"Don't say that," Ted said.

***

"They're past Kearsarge," Robbie said, watching his app.

"Did the off-roaders make it where they needed to be?" Morgan asked.

"I don't know. Hope so." Just at that moment, their phones dinged. Morgan got to hers first.

"Ted. Off-roaders got out of sight in time. Waiting for rest of the enemy convoy to get past that spot, then they'll get on the westbound side of the road and head down."

"That's going to be very dangerous," Robbie said. "Wouldn't want to trade places. They have no armor."

"I know, it's scary as hell. They're fast, at least."

"Doesn't help that much when you have machine guns firing at you," Robbie said. "The only thing that will protect them is the trees at the side of the westbound lanes. Thank God there's no guard rails along there, so they can get into the forest before they have to engage the enemy."

"Yeah, could you imagine if it was the eastbound side, and they were trapped on the highway? That would be a shooting gallery for the enemy."

"They just passed the Baxter overpass," Robbie said.

"So Ted and Justin can probably see them."

"I hope they can only hear them," Robbie said. "These battle wagons are well known to the enemy now."

"Good point. Where's the tail end of the enemy convoy?"

"A mile east of Kearsarge," Robbie said. "They've compacted a lot, though. Good chance they'll be completely inside the kill zone before we have the front end flying off the bridge here."

"What could go wrong? What should we worry about?"

"Too many of them getting out of their vehicles and overpowering us," Robbie said. "They have the numbers. The leaders just passed Crystal Springs Road."

"Won't be long now," she said. "Glad we're just going back far enough to get a clean shot at the road."

"We'll have to watch for RPGs," Robbie said. "Hopefully we can hit the first few rows with enough grenade and mini-gun fire to shock them into submission."

Morgan glanced over at him. "We won't be able to use the rear machine guns as well from where we'll be."

"They've got plenty of range and a good targeting system," Robbie said. "We'll use them to good effect, trust me."

"How close?"

"Any second now," Robbie said.

Suddenly they heard the crash of vehicles hitting the cement below the broken bridge, and the squealing of tires as vehicles tried to stop in a panic.

Robbie and Morgan looked at each other. "Time to go!" Robbie said, getting behind the wheel. He fired up the engine and backed up quickly. "Tell me when you have a clear shot in that sight."

"You got it," Morgan said as she pulled out the tray and looked at the sight. "Keep going, but slow down a little bit."

"Jules is moving."

"Watch the mirrors, not him," Morgan said, "and be ready to angle like we did before."

"Okay."

"There, angle a little more towards the left."

Robbie adjusted. "How's that?"

"Perfect. Get us into siege mode."

Robbie nodded, stopping the coach and hitting the siege mode button. Morgan opened fire, hitting several of the front vehicles right through the windshields.

"That got their attention," she said.

Jules's coach fired rear machine guns too, as Robbie waited for the M19 and mini-gun to rise into place. As soon as the M19 was up he opened fire, shooting a half dozen grenades into the stuck trucks in rapid succession, Jules doing the same. Enemy fighters were leaving their vehicles, trying to run for cover, when the off-roaders fired from the side of the road, blowing up the next several rows of trucks, gas tanks going, spewing fire all over the place.

"It's gonna be tough to hit much more with these rear guns," Morgan said. "We've wasted just about everybody that I can see with the sight."

"I've got a ways to go with the grenade launcher," Robbie said, firing off another half dozen further back, the explosions taking longer to sound. Machine gun fire hit the rear of the coach.

"They're finally shooting back," Morgan said, eyes back on the target reticle. "Stupid." She fired, hitting several men who were lying between ruined vehicles close to the broken edge of the bridge. Several of them were hit, the others trying to crawl backwards as Jules landed two grenades right on top of them, body parts and blood flying into the air. Morgan leaned back from the sight. "That was gross."

"Those off-roaders are still causing havoc, but they're pretty far back there," Robbie said. "Can't see, but I can hear the grenades going off."

"Most of the enemy fighters must be out of their vehicles by now, if they haven't been hit. You haven't even fired the mini-gun yet, have you?"

"Nope, and neither has Jules," Robbie said. "Can't see back far enough now." He fired the grenade launcher several more times, aimed high so they'd fly far. "Hell, I hate using this thing without actually aiming at a target."

"Those trucks are so close together that you're hitting something with almost every shot," she said. More bullets hit the back of the coach, and she fired again, hitting a group of three Islamists who were shooting from prone position behind some of their own dead. Robbie saw them and landed grenades on them. Then a text message came in.

"Who's that?" Morgan asked, eyes glued to the target reticle.

"Ted. They've got the off-ramp completely blocked with broken trucks, and the off-roaders back there are almost out of ammo. He's getting on the escape road."

"Good," Morgan said. There was another ding. "That Tex or Jules?"

"Tex, same thing as Ted, they're leaving."

"Maybe we'd better go too, before more of these folks start climbing out and get a lucky shot at our tires or something."

"Text Jules," Robbie said. "I'm going to light up the end with a bunch of grenade fire and get ready to go."

"On it," she said, sending a quick text to Jules. He replied right away. "They're ready too. He says we should both be firing while we take down siege mode, until we get out of sight."

"Yeah," Robbie said. "It'll keep their heads down." He flipped the switch for siege mode, lowering it as he fired up the mini-gun, sweeping lead across the front of the damaged road, firing a few grenades as well. Then he drove forward quickly, a few stray bullets hitting the back before they were around the bend, Jules right behind them.

"Wow," Morgan said. "Think that did enough good?"

"We'll find out," Robbie said. They squeezed by the roadblock, which the CHP officers had already left behind.

7

Earth Movers

Jules backed into the covered space at the quarry yard. Robbie had already arrived, and a swarm of off-roaders and Jeeps were rolling in. He shut down the engine and got out of his seat, his legs aching from sitting for so long. Sparky got up and stretched.

"Enemy get past bridge?" Jules asked, walking to the dinette, where Shelley and Dana were sitting.

"Not so far," Shelley said, eyes glued to the laptop screen. "I see a lot of them going east on foot."

"We ruined their whole day," Dana said.

"I'm a little worried about the people who live there," Sparky said. "Looks like some of the enemy fighters are pretty close to the escape road."

Shelley nodded. "Our guys should be well beyond those spots."

"I text them now," Jules said, pulling out his phone.

"How many enemy fighters are moving?" Sparky asked.

"Well over half," Shelley said. "From what I can tell. Some are wounded but not dead, of course."

"You mean there's over a hundred thousand enemy fighters roaming around up there?"

"Give or take," Shelley said. "They're in trouble, though. There's not much nearby. They need a Dunkirk operation to get them out of harm's way."

"It's cold at night now," Sparky said. "If they don't have shelter, they're gonna have a hard night. Would've been easier for them a month ago."

"Ted, Tex, and others out of area," Jules said. "Some action on way out, Ted's mini gun turret damaged. Several off-roaders killed on escape road."

"Wonder how many off-roaders we lost?" Dana asked.

"Hope not many," Jules said. "Sparky, you know terrain, weather patterns there?"

"Yeah, spent a lot of time there in my twenties," Sparky said. "On fire crews, and on vacations. It gets cold at night, but some of them are from climates that get cold too. Afghanistan, for instance."

"They'll build fires," Shelley said. "Try to keep alive. I think Ivan's team should recruit up there. If the Islamists don't have an easy way out, they'll hurt lots of people as they walk away. We'll see raids, and a lot of civilians killed."

"I'll text Ivan," Jules said. "Need to update him on operation anyway."

"You know, if we have a whole bunch of people starting campfires there, we'll have a dangerous situation," Sparky said.

"Dangerous how?" Dana asked.

"We had a dry year. The place is like a tinder box. A forest fire could create a lot of havoc for them."

"Ivan call in few minutes," Jules said. "Busy at moment."

"There's Tex and Cody coming in the gate," Sparky said.

"Good," Dana said. "Ted and Justin ought to be coming within fifteen minutes or so."

"That right, based on text from Ted," Jules said. His phone rang. He put it on speaker and set it on the dinette table, then slid onto the seat next to Shelley. "Ivan?"

"Hello, Jules," he said. "We saw what you did on the satellite feed."

"You have satellite feed back now?"

"Yes," he said. "The Feds are losing control of everything. How'd you guys kill so many enemy fighters? Looks like you took out nearly half of them."

"Cars and trucks fragile," Jules said. "Grenades burn them fast. Cause chain reaction when they explode. Many never got out of vehicles."

"What's on your mind?"

"There over hundred thousand creeps wandering around there," Jules said. "We need to warn nearby residents. Maybe recruit them to fight."

Ivan chuckled. "Ben Dover started that before you guys got there. We can't field anywhere near a hundred thousand citizens, but we'll have a lot of snipers there. Good marksmen who know the terrain. I wouldn't want to be an enemy fighter out there."

"Excellent," Dana said.

"Are all your people back?" Ivan asked.

"All except last group, and I text with them five minutes ago," Jules said. "Should be here any minute. Ted's coach has damaged mini gun turret."

"How many off-roaders did we lose?"

"Don't know yet, boss. Some. Not many."

"Good," Ivan said. "Rest overnight. We need you in the south. You leave in the morning."

"Ji-Ho all right?" Jules asked.

"He's fine, but there's a huge number of enemy troops massing near the border, as we discussed earlier."

"A few battle wagons aren't going to make much difference," Sparky said.

"Many thousands of recruits will arrive at Dodge City, where Ji-Ho's team is now. They'll need help to manage the situation and work strategy."

"Are there still seven hundred thousand coming?" Shelley asked.

"They're moving five-hundred thousand to the border as we speak, and the two-hundred thousand from northern California are taking the eastern route to link up with them. They're by the Salton Sea right now."

"How many recruits can we count on?" Sparky asked.

"We're counting on a million," Ivan said.

"What?" Sparky asked. "You're high."

Ivan chuckled. "We have a third of those committed already, and we've been given permission to recruit in western San Diego County."

"Who gave that?" Jules asked.

"The US Navy Base commander," Ivan said.

"How far from the border are the enemy fighters?" Sparky asked.

"About sixty miles, but they're on foot."

"We won't make it in time," Sparky said.

"You're probably right, you won't make it there by the time the initial incursion starts," Ivan said, "but there will be plenty for you to do. The battle isn't to keep them from coming over the border. No way to stop that now. The battle will happen inside California. That gives us a lot more time to work with."

"Hey, here comes Ted and Cody's rigs!" Sparky said, watching them through the front windshield. "Right on time."

"Excellent," Ivan said. "I've got to go, but we'll probably have a brief meeting a little later. Be ready to leave at first light tomorrow. Fantastic job. Please relay my praise to all."

The call ended.

"Well, there you have it," Sparky said.

"Let's have quick meeting with others," Jules said, standing up. "Then relax, rest. Tomorrow big day."

***

Saladin was riding shotgun in a nondescript white van, on I-10 just past Banning, heading for the Mexican border. Twelve of his closest men were in the back, along with their weapons and ammo. His phone rang. He sighed when he saw Daan's name, and put it to his ear.

"Hello."

"You stupid son of a bitch," Daan said, his fury coming over the line like lightning.

"Calm down," Saladin said. "What's wrong?"

"You sent men over the Sierras to attack Sacramento without consulting me first?"

"I still command my own men," he said, sweat breaking out on his forehead.

"Yeah, well that wasn't too bright," Daan said. "How did that operation do?"

"I should be hearing from my commanders any time. They should be out of the mountains by now."

Daan laughed sarcastically. "You don't even know, do you?"

"What?"

"Almost half of your men are dead, and the rest are stuck in those mountains with no way out."

"That's impossible. There was no force around large enough to pull that off."

"Didn't take a large force," Daan said. "Ivan's team used a choke point. Blew a small bridge, then trapped your convoy when the leaders got there. Hit their ranks with automatic grenade fire."

"It can't be," Saladin said.

"Those men were working the General Hogan campaign, and now they're dead or stranded," Daan said. "You've just given Hogan a huge gift. It might be our undoing."

"Nonsense," Saladin said, loosening his collar. "It's a minor setback at best. I'll get some men up there to retrieve the survivors."

"No you won't," Daan said. "They'll all be dead by the time you get people there, and the citizens will be strong enough to take them on. You just closed one of the few back doors we have into California. Closed it tighter than a drum."

"We'll make up for it in the south," Saladin said, "unless you think Ivan can come up with a million men."

"He won't need a million men," Daan said. "The Federal Government is headed for trouble, and I'm sure the military knows it."

"I heard that there's another coup attempt in the works. No matter, the real power isn't in the United States anyway."

"That real power you refer to is beginning to fear the US Navy and Air Force using their full capability without fear of Washington," Daan said. "We're in a lot of trouble. The EU Leadership has ordered me to sideline you. You are to report to the base at Capital Reef."

"And if I refuse?"

"I'll have you killed," Daan said.

"My forces will turn on you," Saladin spat.

"I wouldn't count on that."

"I'm going south to run the operation. Everybody's waiting for me."

Daan chuckled. "Seriously, don't do it. Go hide out in Capitol Reef. This will blow over after a while, and then we can attempt to pick up the pieces."

"Who's going to run the operation, then?"

"The lower-level commanders have already been notified, but we need you to verify it."

"Why would I do that?" Saladin asked.

"Because you know that's the only way you'll survive, and be able to get back into this battle."

"There's nothing I can do at Capitol Reef that hasn't already been done," Saladin said.

"We're getting intelligence reports about the Militia. There's been overtures made to them by General Hogan's forces. We need somebody there to hold our alliance together."

Saladin closed his eyes, fighting his emotions back. "That is important. Okay, I can make the case to them. It was I who brought them in originally. I'll do as you ask."

"Good," Daan said. "Take the men you're leading south."

"They aren't needed for the border operation? That's nearly two hundred thousand men."

"We have over seven hundred thousand converging on the border, and another couple hundred thousand on the way to Mazatlán as we speak. The EU Navy is helping with that effort now."

"You're afraid we'll lose California," Saladin said.

Daan was silent for a moment.

"You still there?"

"If we can keep the US Navy's air power out of this, we'll probably win. Yesterday morning I believed they weren't going to be an issue. Now I'm not so sure."

"That was part of the reason I wanted to keep up the pressure in Northern California," Saladin said.

"Finally, some honesty," Daan said. "If we lose this, neither of us will survive. Even if we get out of the country. Our own side will kill us."

"I'll disappear into the woodwork. I've done it before."

Daan laughed. "Good luck with that."

"Where are you?"

"North of Arizona," he said.

"Understood," Saladin said. "Talk to you later."

"Maybe," Daan said. The call ended.

Saladin looked at his driver. "Turn around, and get on I-15. Go northeast."

The driver looked at him nervously and nodded, as Saladin focused on his phone, sending texts.

***

The Saloon in Dodge City was filling up fast, the windows open again, letting in the heat of late afternoon. Ji-Ho was working the audio-visual with Clem, others gathered around chatting. Seth and Kaitlyn were in front of their laptop on a table against the back wall, Angel, Megan, Trevor, and Kaylee sitting with them, eyeing the growing crowd nervously.

"Wonder what's up?" Trevor asked.

"My uncle looks nervous," Kaylee said. "I don't think he's feeling all that well, either."

Garrett came in with Anna and several others, followed by Ed and Tyler. Sam brought in Mia, Erica arriving a few minutes later with Sarah, Yvonne, and Sid.

Ji-Ho stood before the crowd. "Thank you all for coming. We expect conference call with Ivan and others in five minutes. Just relax. Find seats. Make room for others."

"The fire department wouldn't like this," Willard cracked from behind the bar, a grin on his face. "Too bad I'm not serving. Make a pretty penny."

"Oh, shut up, you old goat," Susanne said.

"Be nice, honey," Elmer said.

She rolled her eyes and sat next to him. "You shut up too. Like living with teenagers."

"What'd you do now, guys?" Garrett whispered.

"I heard that," Susanne said. "They found more booze down in the tunnel. Decided to mess with that instead of fixing my lights. Want me to use candles down there to work by?"

"We've got enough modern weapons now," Elmer said. "We don't need you breaking your back loading black powder rounds anymore."

"Yeah, we're good, until we run out," she said. "I'm still gonna keep working."

"We have people coming on now," Ji-Ho said. The screen came up, split three ways. Ivan was on the left, Ben Dover in the center, and Jules, Ted, Sparky, and Tex crowding into the right.

"Well I'll be damned," Sam said, looking at his old friends. "How's it going, guys?"

Ted smiled. "Figures. In a bar. Some things never change."

"Hi, men," Ji-Ho said. "So great to see you."

"We'll have some social time soon enough," Ivan said. "We need to get this over with quickly. Everybody hear me okay?"

"No problem in saloon," Ji-Ho said.

"Same here," Jules said.

"We hear you," Ben Dover said, a few members of his team popping their heads out behind him.

"Okay, here's the situation. We all know that there's three quarters of a million enemy troops massing south of the border, on foot. They've got about two days of walking to get to the California border."

"Yeah, been watching them on the apps," Ed said. Others agreed, in the saloon and on the screen.

"We've also got a couple hundred thousand on the way south from Northern California," Ivan said. "That's the bad news."

"There's good news?" Sam asked.

"We've got nearly that many recruits on the way," Ivan said, "but thanks to your handiwork early in the war, it's not easy to get them from where they are to where we need them."

"You're talking about the pass we blew up on Highway 94," Sid said.

"Precisely," Ivan said. "We need that opened up, and have a convoy of earth movers and massive bull dozers heading to the scene now."

"Got a month?" Sam asked.

"You don't understand," Ivan said. "We've got enough equipment coming to clear your mess in a few days."

"Where did you get it?" Sid asked. "I know what we'd need, and it's a lot, trust me."

"San Diego County had everything that we needed, including the crews who are experienced with this sort of problem. They're stepping in."

"Okay, so we take three days to clear that out," Ed said. "That will be just in time for the enemy troops to use it as a gateway into San Diego."

"You're right, we won't have that mess cleared before the enemy gets over the border," Ivan said. "All that means is that we'll be fighting them on our home turf, and we'll have some help."

"Help?" Ji-Ho asked.

"The US Navy's aviators are going to join us," Ivan said. "In large numbers. We'll get help from the Marines as well."

"How much air power do they have that's not out on a carrier someplace?" Ted asked.

"A lot more than I expected," Ivan said. "And there are two carriers on the way into the general area as we speak. The carriers might be a little late to the party, but we probably won't need them."

"What general area?" Ji-Ho asked.

"The Pacific coast of Southern California," Ivan said. "Don't put that on the internet, please."

There were murmurs in the room.

"So, what's our role?" Sam asked.

"We'd like to set up Dodge City as a way station and supply depot for this operation," Ivan said.

"That puts a big target on us," Garrett said.

"That's why we're talking," Ivan said. "It does make you a target, but you won't be alone, and you'll have capability that is vastly superior to what you have now. We are poised to terrorize the enemy and destroy them. This is the beginning of the end."

"And where will you be during this?" Sam asked.

"There with you, if you'll allow it," Ivan said. "Jules and his team are also on the way to you."

"Old home week," Sam said.

"What does that mean, daddy?" Mia asked.

"It means some old, dear friends are going to join us, sweetie," Sam said.

"You've got a daughter, partner?" Tex asked.

"Yep," he said.

"Social later," Ivan said. "I do not command you people. I'm running this by you all. Are there objections to the moves I'm suggesting?"

"I'm for it, as long as it work," Ji-Ho said. "If help doesn't really come through, we just opened back door to enemy. Millions of innocents are in danger."

"If we don't beat the enemy, they in danger anyway," Jules said. "They just march to I-8."

"He's right," Sam said. "Highway 94 isn't even half the capacity of I-8, and there's nothing to stop the enemy from getting on that big road and going full bore into San Diego."

"I'm not hearing any objections," Ivan said.

"Me neither," Garrett said. "I'm for it. Let's do this."

"I agree," Tex said.

"Me too," Sam said.

"Okay, then let's make some detailed plans," Ivan said. "We don't need to have the whole group together to do that."

"Hey, everybody," Seth said, raising his hand. "Something's going on!"

"Who's that?" Ivan asked.

"That's Seth, our data guy," Sam said.

"What do you see, partner?" Tex asked.

"Those two-hundred thousand enemy fighters from the north turned around. They're going northeast. Most of them are on I-15 or heading in that direction."

Ivan laughed.

"What's so funny?" Sam asked.

"I think I know," Jules said, a sly grin on his face.

"Well, are you gonna tell us?" Sam asked.

"My guess is that Saladin has been called back to the Utah base," Ivan said. "He pulled a very stupid move last night, and it cost him a couple hundred thousand fighters."

"What happened?" Sam asked.

"We happened, partner," Tex said, a look of glee on his face.

{8}

Clackers

Tex woke up next to Karen before it was light, not able to sleep anymore. The plans they agreed to last night were spinning through his head like a North-Texas twister.

"Hey," Karen said, turning to face him. "It's early. You okay?"

"Nerves," he said. "I'm fine, though. You can sleep some more. I'm getting up."

"I've got a better idea," she said, sitting up and pulling her short nightgown over her head. Tex smiled as she covered him. "My breath might be a little rotten."

"I don't care," he said, his arms going around her. They made love quietly but passionately, ending up on their backs, Tex's right hand intertwined with her left.

"What are we gonna do after the war?" Karen asked, turning her head towards his.

"I haven't had time to give it much thought," he said. "You have some ideas?"

"Do you think we'll last together after it?"

Tex chuckled. "Still?"

"Still what?"

"You're still doubting our relationship?" Tex asked.

"You said we'd be together as long as both of us wants it, remember?"

"And I've said different things since, remember?"

She turned on her side, facing him. "I'm serious."

"What do you want to happen?"

"I asked you first," she said.

He turned on his side towards her, staring into her beautiful face, framed by her thick red hair. "You're really going to make me say it right now?"

She rolled her eyes. "I can tell when you're teasing me, you know."

He smiled, reaching to brush her hair from her eyes. "You're the love of my life. I hoped that would be the case when I was pursuing you. I'm pretty sure now."

"*Pretty* sure?"

He chuckled. "When I say *pretty* it means *very*. You know that. Why do women ask questions about things when they already know the answer?"

"Oh, I don't know. Because we need to, I guess."

"Are you gonna tell me what you want, then?" Tex asked.

She laughed. "You're doing the same thing you just accused me of doing."

"Answer the question," he said with a stern expression.

"I just want to be with you. Whatever direction that takes us is fine with me. It'll be an adventure."

"That wasn't the answer I expected," he said.

"Oh, you think I've got this vision of what our life together will be?"

"We've been living our lives together for a while now."

"We've been *on the run* together. When this is over we won't be on the run anymore."

He sat up and scratched his head. "What makes you think we're gonna settle down into some boring relationship?"

"Do you think that's what I want?"

He laid back down. "No, that's *not* what I think you want. I can't tell if you want me to be serious or romantic or both."

She laughed again. "You do know how that came out, right?"

"You're not going to get mad, are you?"

She elbowed him, on the verge of laughter. "Living with you won't be boring, I suspect. You're right, I don't want the little house with the picket fence, and at this point I'm not that interested in having a bunch of kids."

"Why not?"

"Why not what?" she asked.

"Why not a bunch of kids?"

"We aren't suited for it. Maybe I'll let you knock me up during a weak moment, but I doubt that will happen. We'll have adventures together instead."

"Travel the world, huh. Or *walk the earth.*"

She rolled her eyes. "Stop with the Tarantino references. I had a boyfriend who worshiped him. Don't be that guy."

Tex laughed. "Who's Tarantino?"

She elbowed him again. "Stop it. Do you want kids?"

"At this point in my life, I just want you. Fully and completely. If life leads us to having kids and we both want it, I'm down, but neither of us know if that's going to happen."

"What about the big M?"

"I told you I'd do that," Tex said.

"You're not sure about anything long term, but you'd marry me?"

"Yes," he said, getting out of bed.

"Where are you going?"

"We're leaving early, remember?"

She pulled the covers back, revealing herself to him, smiling at his reaction. "Sure you're in such a hurry?"

"Yep, and you know we have to be," he said. "You're waiting for me to say something, but I'm not sure what that is."

She shook her head, looking a little frustrated, and got out of bed.

"You're really getting upset," he said, walking to her. He took her into his arms. "You're afraid that when the battle is over, I'll lose interest in you. In us."

"Sorry," she said, looking up at him, her arms going around his waist.

"I'm not going anywhere. I want to be with you for the rest of my life. That's not going to change. We'll live out our lives doing the things that make us happy. For me, that's going to include getting married."

She held him tighter. "Why do you care about being married?"

"Maybe I want the exclusivity that it forces," he said. "Maybe I want us to own each other. Or maybe I'm just a romantic Texan who has more traditional values than I care to admit."

She turned her head, resting it on his chest, holding him tighter still.

"You okay?"

"I'm happy," she said. "I've got the man I've always dreamed of." She broke the hug. "Okay, you can get dressed now."

She turned towards her dresser and got out clothes, as he watched her, shaking his head.

They had a quick cup of coffee, watching out the window as the off-roaders loaded backpacks onto their vehicles, getting ready to go.

"I'm gonna unhook the utilities," Tex said, heading for the door.

"Okay, I'll stow things," Karen said, making eye contact. "Thank you."

He tipped his hat and disappeared through the door. After a second there was a soft rap on the side of the coach.

"Yes?" Karen asked.

"It's me," Shelley said.

"Hey, come on up. I'm about done. You guys ready to go?"

"Yeah," Shelly said, climbing the steps. She had on a tight-fitting t-shirt and jeans. "Tex had a smile as big as Texas."

"We were chatting about after the war. I can't believe I resisted that man. He's a jewel."

"He is," she said, sitting on the couch.

"Okay, what's up?" Karen asked, eyeing her.

"You can't tell anybody," she whispered.

"I have an idea."

"I think I'm pregnant," Shelley said. "Just had to tell somebody."

"You sure?"

"Pretty sure, but I'll get one of those test kits when we get a chance."

"Does Jules know?"

"No," Shelley said, "and don't tell him. I want to wait until I'm sure, but I'm just going crazy."

"Your secret is safe with me," Karen said.

"Hey, Shelley, you guys ready to go?" Tex asked as he came back into the coach.

"Yep, we're ready," Shelley said. "I'd better get back over there. Talk to you later, Karen."

"Bye," Karen said.

"See you, Tex," Shelley said, shooting him a smile on the way out.

Tex got behind the wheel and started the engine. "What was that all about?"

"Oh, nothing, just girl talk," Karen said.

"Uh huh." Tex shot her a sidelong glance. "The gate is opening. Time to go."

Karen sat in the passenger seat, watching Tex as she put her seatbelt on. "I love you."

"I love you too, little lady."

***

Jacumba Hot Springs had become a mini-metropolis. Every flat spot in town was covered with parked cars, and the wilderness between the town and the fortified stretch of Old Highway 80 was covered with tents of every shape and size. Truckloads of weapons had been coming down the highway, and there were men with the trucks to teach citizens how to use them.

"Where's all this stuff coming from?" Doug asked.

"Yeah, that's what I'd like to know," Jorge said.

Conrad smiled. "All over. We've got some Marines showing up in a few minutes."

"They gonna fight with us?" Doug asked.

"Oh, they'll be fighting, but I'm not sure if they'll be here or not. This is a supply and training visit."

"We've already been trained with the M60s, M19s, and a lot of other stuff," Jorge said. "What else is there?"

"You ever heard of the M18A1 Claymore mine?" Conrad asked.

"We're gonna mine the area?" Doug asked.

"Yeah, but these aren't like your normal mines. They're anti-personnel weapons. Good when you have a massive number of enemy fighters heading your way."

"Maybe that's them coming right now," Jorge said, pointing to a military truck coming towards them from town. Conrad stepped forward and motioned to a parking place. Citizen fighters moved out of the way to let the truck pass. It parked, and the cab doors opened, two men getting out and walking over.

"Are you Conrad Kowalski?" asked the older of the two, a man in his thirties with a muscular build and a square jaw.

"I am," Conrad said.

"Good. I'm Corporal Callahan, and this is Private First-Class Alito. We're here to provide training for the M18A1 Claymore mine. Do you have men picked out to receive the training?"

"Haven't gotten to that. How many men do you need?"

"For a deployment of this size, twelve would be optimum," he said.

"I'm willing to be a trainee," Doug said.

"Me too," Jorge said.

"I'm good with that," Conrad said. "Both of you learn fast. I have ten others in mind. I'll be back in a few minutes."

He turned and left, coming back in less than five minutes with the other men.

Callahan was looking at the border fence through binoculars. "We'll need to be on the other side of that. Does somebody here have the key?"

"Yes sir," Conrad said. "I got it from the border patrol. Do we need a place to drive that truck through? There's a larger break in the K-rail line about fifty yards east of here."

"That would be helpful," Callahan said. "Let's go. You can ride in the cab, the others can climb in the back, but don't mess with the crates. Understand?"

"Yes," Conrad said, looking at the others. "You heard the man."

The men climbed into the back of the truck as Conrad followed the Marines to the cab. They backed out and went down the road, turning off between two K-rails, heading for the gate in the border fence and parking there. Everybody got out, and Conrad unlocked the gate. He pushed it open, the rusted hinges moaning.

"Thank you," Callahan said. "First we'll talk about the weapons. Let's gather around the back of the truck. Alito, get in there and grab me one."

"Yes sir," Alito said, his wiry frame jumping inside. He came back with a canvas bag, about the size of a large purse, sliding it to the edge of the truck.

"Normally we use this bandoleer to carry the weapon in the field," Callahan said. He opened the flap on the top and pulled out a curved rectangular item, olive drab in color, with the embossed words Front Toward Enemy on the convex side. It had folding spikes on the bottom, two ports on the top, and a sight between the ports. "This is the mine. It's C-4 plastic explosive behind ball bearings, which are set in epoxy. When the C-4 is detonated, the ball bearings fly forward in an expanding pattern, going out as far as 250 meters, but at that range it's not optimum. We'll place these to get the most effective range, which is about fifty meters."

"Sounds like a shotgun," Doug said.

"That's about it," Alito said.

"How many ball bearings?" one of Conrad's men asked.

"About seven hundred," Alito said.

Jorge stepped up to take a closer look. "It's not very big, is it?"

Alito grinned. "No, but it packs a good punch."

Callahan smirked, then pulled two more items from the bandoleer: a long wire, wrapped around a rectangular spool, and a metal item with an electrical plug and a lever over a cylindrical button, which he held up next. "This is the M57 detonator. We call it the clacker. You plug one end of the wire into this port, and the other end of the wire to the blasting cap assembly, which is installed on the mine. Note the safety arm, which will go in place like this, to prevent the lever from pushing down on the detonator button." He worked it in front of the men.

"Where's the blasting cap?" Doug asked.

"Inside the spool for the wire," Callahan said, picking it up and removing the blasting cap assembly from one end. "We'll be using a daisy chain to connect the mines together in several rows."

"How long is that wire?" Jorge asked.

"One hundred feet," Alito said.

"Yes, and that makes this a dangerous job," Callahan said. "We'll set these up in staggered rows, starting a hundred meters from those hills out there, and bringing them in about one hundred meters for each row. We should have enough to cover the entire area on the Mexican side of the fence, and at least one row on our side. The last of the detonations will be from behind the K-rail you have set up there. Nice job, by the way."

"That's it?" Jorge asked.

"That's the gist," Callahan said. "Alito, take the men out with forty mines and set them up about a hundred meters this side of those hills."

"Yes sir," Alito said, climbing back into the truck. "Somebody come give me a hand."

Several men climbed in and helped him load the first forty bandoleers onto the back end of the truck, then the men picked up three or four each and followed Private Alito through the gate. Conrad stayed behind with Callahan.

"How far are the enemy fighters now?" Callahan asked.

Conrad pulled his phone out and fired up the app, focusing on it and then showing it to Callahan. "Forty-five miles. They're moving slower than we expected."

"That's what I saw this morning," Callahan said. "They're slowing down because they're waiting for something. That might not be good for us."

"Did they give you guys the apps?"

Callahan chuckled. "They're working on it. They need to buy a whole lot of smart phones. Damn military wouldn't let us just use our own."

"What's to stop you from doing that anyway?"

Callahan pulled his phone out of his pocket. "Nothing, but I've been told not to encourage that. All my men have them, but if you tell my CO I'll deny I knew about it."

Conrad laughed. "Not much different than it was when I was in."

"Marines?"

"No, Army," Conrad said.

"If they really throw a half-million men at this line, these mines will slow them down for a very short period of time. You know that, right?"

"Yeah, I know that," Conrad said. "We'll have thousands of men up here with M60s and M19s. We're already making plans on how to proceed when we're close to being overrun, though."

"What are you going to do?"

Conrad smiled. "We have the cars arranged so we can get into them and live to fight another day," he said. "Helps that the enemy is on foot. The mines will help some, but they also complicate matters. We'll probably lose the first few men we have on the detonation line."

"If they're fast, they might survive," Callahan said. "You'll need to dig trenches for all of the detonation spots except the last one behind the K-rails. When these things go off they scare the crap out of everybody who isn't killed outright, which should give our guys enough time to get through that gate and under cover before the next wave goes off. Know anything about the quality of the men we're up against?"

"No, not really," Conrad said. "They might be getting down to the dregs."

"Or they might finally be putting their best into the fight," Callahan said.

"Yeah. You think we'll really get a million citizens recruited?"

"I was gonna ask you that."

"I wish I knew," Conrad said. "Been pleasantly surprised so far. We've got some good folks."

"We've been arguing with the brass for a while now about joining the fight with Ivan the Butcher."

"Why wouldn't they?" Conrad asked. "I get that question every ten minutes."

Callahan shook his head in disgust. "Job one for the brass is to ensure that no more foreigners get involved, no matter what the damage to the civilian population."

"Foreigners as in the EU or the UN?"

Callahan laughed. "You guys pretty much kicked the UN out of here. All they have left is stragglers, from what our sources are saying, and the EU stopped funding the UN. It's unlikely we'll get more."

"Good, then we might be out of the woods soon."

"There's a lot more Islamists in the pipeline," Callahan said. "Half of the fighters we've seen here came from other parts of the world they've infiltrated. Mostly the European countries. *Refugees.* Their leadership figured that experience would help them here."

"That's a big fail," Conrad said. "This ain't Europe. Our people are different."

"You'd think they would know that. Anyway, there's a fair number of enemy fighters coming from the middle east now. More than we've had before. Don't know if that's better or worse for us."

"Why isn't the Navy targeting their transport ships?"

"Same reason they wouldn't let us help you guys," Callahan said. "They're afraid the EU is going to lead a big foreign intervention."

"We'll mop the floor with those Eurotrash punks," Conrad said.

"Good, keep that attitude. I think you're right on the money, by the way. I've seen what the citizens have done. Here, in Texas, and all over the Southwest. Brings tears to my eyes, and that's the truth."

"I was impressed by the people in Oregon," Conrad said. "Didn't expect that."

"I did. That's where I'm from."

"Well, they got the first row placed," Conrad said, watching the men approach the truck for a new load. "What about air support?"

"The Navy brass doesn't want to bomb Mexico. They'll hold off until the enemy has crossed the border."

"That's not too bright," Conrad said. "It'll get a lot of these people killed."

"Preaching to the choir," Callahan said.

{9}

Three Roads

Sid drove the Jeep towards the break in the fence behind Dodge City, Clem next to him with the surveillance equipment.

"We'll have to hurry," Sid said. "It'll be dark soon."

"Yeah, I'd like to be out of here before then," Yvonne said from the back seat, her rifle cradled in her lap. "I feel like our butts are hanging out on the line. There could be snipers on any of those ridges up there."

"Garrett's men are still patrolling," Sid said.

"That's what they're saying, but have you seen one out here yet?" Yvonne asked.

"They're probably on the other side of the ridges," Sid said.

"Don't worry," Clem said. "This won't take long. There's the spot. Got here faster than I expected."

"Helps to know where you can go fast," Sid said, "and helps not to be worried about looking for tracks."

"True, that slowed us way down the first time we came," Yvonne said.

Sid parked the Jeep next to the fence, several feet to the left of the break, and hopped out, Clem following. Yvonne stayed in the back of the Jeep, putting the binoculars to her eyes and scanning the ridges.

"Something doesn't feel right," Sid said, slowing as he approached the fence break. "Hold it. Look at the ground there."

Clem stopped, squinting as he looked. "What?"

"Somebody's disturbed the dirt," he whispered.

"Maybe it was Garrett's patrol."

"I don't see any hoof prints. No foot prints either. Looks like that dirt has been brushed."

"Maybe it was wild life," Clem said, walking towards the break.

"Stop," Sid said. "Stay back." He crept up to the spot, looking down. He could see scrape marks on the dirt, fading due to the wind, but still visible.

"What do you think?" Clem asked.

"I think somebody put a land mine or two here."

"Dammit. What should we do?"

"Get way back in the Jeep and have Yvonne fire at it with her rifle," Sid said. "C'mon."

They trotted back to the Jeep.

"Something's wrong," Yvonne said.

"Looks like there's a mine placed in that break," he said. "One of you text Garrett and make sure none of his men did it while I move us back."

"I'm on it," Clem said, taking out his phone. He sent a text as Sid started the jeep and drove back about sixty yards.

"What are we gonna do?" Yvonne asked.

"I want you to fire at the dirt once we're back far enough, unless Garrett tells us that they set the mine there."

"Sure it's a mine?"

"Well, they buried something there," Sid said. "Might take more than one shot to blow it."

"Garrett just got back to me. It wasn't them. I asked him why we aren't seeing his patrols around here. He sounded real worried. There's more folks on the way now."

Sid stopped the Jeep. "This ought to do it. Start taking pot shots."

"Turn around facing it so I can use the roll bar as a rest," she said.

Sid nodded and turned the Jeep around. Yvonne rested her rifle on the roll bar and aimed, pulling the trigger. The bullet pelted the ground, but nothing happened.

"You sure it's a mine?" Clem asked.

"Those things have a detonator button. Might take a few tries to hit it."

"We might just break the assembly, and never touch it off," Yvonne said. "I'll try a few more shots. You guys keep your eyes on the ridges. There might be somebody up there."

She fired several more times, hitting the spot, no explosion going off. Then there was the crack of a rifle shot, Yvonne dropping immediately as a bullet hit the roll bar.

"You hit?" Sid shouted.

"No," she said. "Roll out of the Jeep. It came from the right."

"I see where they came from," Clem said, nodding towards his right. "They're gonna get me before I can get behind something."

"I see them," Sid said, pulling out his rifle. Another shot rang out, hitting the side of the Jeep, then another, popping one of the tires. Sid fired several times, causing the snipers to get down.

"Now!" Sid said, scrambling behind the Jeep as Clem and Yvonne did the same, all of them with weapons in hand.

"Text Garrett again," Sid said, reaching into the back of the Jeep as another shot rang out, hitting the front windshield.

Clem did that, as Yvonne watched the ridge where the snipers head was popping up every few seconds. She tried to time his rhythm, firing at the right time, splitting the sniper's head. "Got the bastard."

"Nice shot, baby," Sid said, pulling his M60 in front of him. He aimed at the break in the gate and fired, the stream of bullets setting off several mines, one of them a few feet in front of the gate break.

"Whoa, I was almost on top of that one," Clem said, looking over at Sid.

"You get Garrett?"

"Yeah, I let him know what was going on. I told him we needed a ride."

Another shot rang out, from behind them this time.

"Dammit," Yvonne said, rushing for cover with the others, then aiming again, watching the ridge. "Come on out, slug."

"This is why I love her," Sid quipped.

"Focus, dammit," Yvonne said, pulling the trigger, tagging the sniper in the neck.

"Wow," Clem said, clutching his rifle.

"These are more UN folks," Sid said. "We would've gotten buzzed by the apps if they weren't."

"Thought we'd nailed most of them," Yvonne said.

"There might only be a few of them out here, and we've killed two already," Clem said, his eyes peeled. "It's gonna be dark soon."

Gunfire erupted from behind the ridge, a mixture of M60 automatic fire and black powder rounds, the smoke starting to drift into the air. It went on for several minutes, AK-47s returning fire for a few moments. Then there was silence.

"I'd say that was more than a few," Yvonne said.

"Horses on the ridge," Clem said, pointing.

Sid reached into the back of the Jeep for the binoculars and put them to his eyes, straining in the low light of dusk. "We just got an all-clear sign."

"Thank God," Yvonne said. "We still gonna place these damn cameras?"

"We should do it now, while we still have some light," Clem said.

"We need to be careful over there," Sid said. "Might be more mines."

"Yeah," Yvonne said.

"I'll be fine," Clem said, "but do me a favor. Stay here and fix the flat, so we can leave."

"I think I ought to go with you," Sid said.

"No," Yvonne said. "Change the tire. I'll watch for both of you."

Sid nodded and got to work, as Clem grabbed the box of surveillance cameras and hurried back to the fence. He watched the ground as he neared, his flashlight pointed at the dirt around the broken spot.

"Good, he's being careful," Sid said as he put the jack under the Jeep.

"More horses on the ridge, over where the first shots came from."

Their phones dinged. Sid pulled his and looked. "Garrett said three of his patrolmen were killed, and there were twelve UN Peacekeepers behind that ridge."

"Dammit," Yvonne said. "This sucks."

Clem placed the cameras, one on the tree facing the outside, others on the fence posts themselves, on either side of the break. He looked at the crater. There was the edge of an unexploded mine visible on the other side of the fence. He texted Sid about it.

"What did he see?" Yvonne asked when she heard the ding.

"There's an unexploded mine sticking part way in the dirt, beyond the fence."

"Are we gonna fire at it?"

Sid sent another text to Garrett. "Let's see what Garrett wants us to do."

His phone dinged after a moment.

"Well?" Yvonne asked.

"He said to leave it," Sid said, "in case they think they all got blown up. He's going to spread the word to stay away from here."

Clem rushed back to the Jeep as Sid was pulling the old tire off.

"How much longer?" he asked.

"Five minutes," Sid said. "Might want to cancel our ride."

"Don't," Yvonne said. "Just in case. They can escort us home."

"Yeah, I agree," Clem said.

Sid nodded and finished installing the spare. "Good thing I just put air in this." He stowed the jack. "Let's go."

They got in and Sid drove them home, meeting several other Jeeps on the way, who turned and followed them.

***

"Stockton is always bigger than I remember," Shelley said, in the passenger seat of the battle wagon. Jules was at the wheel, Sparky and Dana on the couch.

"I hope using I-5 to go south was the right idea," Dana said. "Lots of people on this road. These battle wagons are easy to spot."

"Most people don't know," Jules said. "Glad we fixed Ted's mini gun gimbal. With gun out, people tell, no?"

Sparky laughed. "Yeah, that's for sure, although most people who see us are probably on our side."

"One would hope," Dana said. "We're not taking this all the way down, are we?"

"The boss asked that we get on I-15 before we get too far south," Jules said. "Navy don't want caravan through coastal side of San Diego."

Sparky chuckled. "Yeah, I could see that, I guess. Are we going into Dulzura using Highway 94?"

"That the plan," Jules said. "Should work. Long drive. Wish we could spend a night on way."

"We've got four drivers," Shelley said. "We should keep going."

Dana was looking at her phone. "Here's how to go. Get on the 210 Freeway at Sylmar, then take that down to I-15."

"That's a good idea," Sparky said. "Been that route before."

Jules shrugged. "Okay, I do. How many hours?"

"Says eight hours and seventeen minutes from Stockton, which we just passed," Dana said. "It's not that bad, and all of our rigs have more than one driver."

"Some of the off-roaders don't," Sparky said.

"They make detour anyway," Jules said, "weapons upgrades being done in Santa Clarita."

"At the same place we picked the battle wagons up?" Shelley asked.

"Yep," Jules said.

"Are you sure that's safe?" Dana asked.

"Enemy never found," Jules said. "Should be good. They spend night, changes take time."

"Hope we don't lose a bunch of them," Sparky said. "We're gonna need them, I think."

They settled into the drive, not speaking much for many miles, Dana finally laying on the couch and dozing, Sparky stretching out on the dinette bench and nodding off.

"You no sleep?" Jules asked, glancing at Shelley.

"Oh, I'm okay," she said. "It really feels like we'll get to the end of this soon."

"Good chance, but dangers ahead. You know this."

"Yes, I know," she said. "Anxious to see your old friends?"

"Very much. Ji-Ho and Sam are fun. You'll like."

She smiled at him. "Ji-Ho reminds me of a big kid."

"Yes," Jules said. "He got idea for battle wagons."

"I heard, from that guy named George."

Jules smiled. "Yes, George. Too bad he not with."

"We should decide where to trade off drivers," Shelley said, pulling her phone in front of her face.

"Bakersfield?"

"Hmmm, that's pretty far," Shelley said, brow furrowed under her blonde hair. "How are you feeling?"

"I good for long time."

"It's almost another three hours away," she said, "and the town would be Buttonwillow. Bakersfield is too far east."

"We can run generator, use coffee maker and microwave," Jules said.

"Yes, we should do that," Shelley said, "unless you want to stop, and I think that would be a bad idea."

"Agree. Maybe you should get shut-eye."

"No, I'm gonna let Sparky drive the next round, and I'm the only person awake other than you right now. I'll stay awake while you're driving, if you don't mind."

"I don't mind," Jules said, glancing at her.

The miles ticked by, the coach silent inside except for muffled road noise and Sparky's snoring. Shelley was thinking about the pregnancy, making plans for getting a test kit, going over her speech to Jules in her mind, the feelings warming her as they cruised in the mid-afternoon sun.

"You in heavy thought," Jules said. "I see wheels turning."

"I suppose you want to know what I'm thinking."

"Your thoughts are your own," Jules said. "Tell me if you want, no pressure, okay?"

"I'm just thinking about our lives after the war, that's all," she said.

"Good thoughts, I hope?"

"Of course, honey," she said.

"USA be mess for months. I hope we can find safe quiet place to ride out."

"Don't you think we'll be looked at as heroes when this is over?" Shelley asked.

"By many, yes. By all, no."

"Who would want the enemy to win?" Shelley asked.

"Leftists who want end to democratic society and nationalism," Jules said. "Fight goes on. Trust me. I expect pressure to break USA into smaller chunks."

"We can't do that."

Jules smiled. "We shouldn't do that. Not same as can't."

"Do you want to stay in America? Or will we go back to Europe?"

"Partly depends on who survives conflict, who control governments," Jules said, "but that's minor, as far as I'm concerned."

"Minor?"

"Yes, biggest issue is where we want to make life together. Joint decision. We both American citizens. We can stay here. Maybe vacation in Europe."

"You'd be okay with that?"

Jules chuckled. "Nicer here. Better society. Less class garbage. Less intrusive government. More rights spelled out in Constitution."

"But your business," she said.

Jules laughed. "I could sell, money in bank more than enough for us and later generations."

"Do you want to sell?"

"We need to think about," he said. "Maybe. Don't have to move there to run business. Have to go more often, though. Might be fine. We'll see."

"If you sold it all, what would you do?" Shelley asked.

"I figure something out," he said. "Not worry me."

"What if you get bored?"

"Then I do something," Jules said. "Opportunities abound. Trust me. This is America, babe."

Shelley was silent for a few minutes, thinking about what he said. "What if we just lived in this for a while? Traveled the countryside. People do that all the time here, you know."

Jules smiled. "I like idea. Might have to remove armaments."

"Wouldn't that be weird? Not having to worry about Islamists or the UN trying to kill us all the time?"

"Life go back to normal after while," he said. "Hope your captivity not too harmful over the years."

"It's just something bad that happened," she said. "Look at all the Jews who were in concentration camps, but went on to normal lives after the war. People can be strong."

"True, and *you* strong," he said. "If ever bother you, we work. Professional help or whatever you need. Understand?"

"Of course, honey. It's not bothering me now. Will it in the future? I don't know. We'll see."

"Checked apps lately?"

Shelley shook her head no. "I'd better, been a while." She picked her phone off the center console and loaded the app.

"Where are we?" Sparky asked, stretching in the dinette.

"We just passed Turk," Shelley said. "We're going to switch drivers when we get to Buttonwillow."

"How long?"

"Hour and a half, give or take," Shelley said. "We should get fuel there too."

"Okay, I'm gonna try to doze a little longer, then."

"Use bedroom if like," Jules said.

"Nah, I can sleep okay here," he said. "Thanks."

"No enemy hits along our route at all," Shelley said. "Still seeing a few to the east, but I think they're going to link up with the group heading to Utah."

"Where east?" Jules asked.

"They're on Highway 395, heading for I-15," she said.

"Where's rest of enemy group?"

"The closest are already past Vegas. The furthest are almost to St. George."

"That Utah?" Jules asked.

"Yep," Shelley said. "We're looking good."

"How about south?"

Shelley moved her fingers on the screen, getting to the border area. "There's way more enemy fighters down there than I like to see."

"How far from border?"

"Hard to tell with this app. Maybe forty miles."

Jules glanced at her, looking worried. "They slow down. Waiting for more forces, perhaps. How many hits south of their position?"

Shelley looked. "Lots more. Thousands. Coming from Mazatlán, but they're way south. They're actually closer to the Texas border than they are to the California border."

"But they head for California, no?"

"That's what it looks like to me," Shelley said. "They're on Mexican Highway 18, which hugs the coast until it goes east into Hermosillo. The rest of the roads to the California border look pretty bad."

"It Mexico," Jules said. "They be on foot eventually. They plan to have vehicles ready for Old Highway 80. We aren't going to make that easy for them."

"Didn't Ivan say they'd overrun our forces at the border?"

"Yes, but we have large buildup of forces at best spot," Jules said. "We slow down while other forces are brought up, and then Naval Aviators show up. Blast to kingdom come."

"There's a lot that can go wrong with that plan."

Jules nodded. "Tell me."

"Well, if they get vehicles on Old Highway 80, they can go to I-8, then head either west into San Diego or east and up further into California. They could also take Old Highway 80 to Highway 94 and roll right up to where we'll be."

"You mention only three roads they can use," Jules said. "Two are tiny and easy to attack. One is bigger but also easy to attack. Old Highway 80, Highway 94, and I-8."

"There's a lot more if they go east on I-8," Shelley said.

"They only go that way if they flee to Arizona," Jules said. "If they go further up into California, we whittle troops down to nothing. Only chance to make difference is San Diego. They will take out Naval Base or die trying. We make sure they die trying."

{10}

The Wire

Sid, Yvonne, and Clem rolled into the back parking area, a block outside of Dodge City's main street.

"What now?" Yvonne asked.

"I could use a snort and some conversation about what just happened," Clem said. "Going to the saloon."

"Sounds kinda good to me," Sid said.

"Mind if I go back to our rig?" Yvonne asked. "I'm tired."

"Sure, no problem," Sid said. "I'll walk you there, change my clothes, and meet Clem back in town. That okay?"

"Sure, but don't get too trashed. We're seeing too much enemy activity around here."

"I think we ought to have the battle wagons in siege mode," Clem said.

"Me too," Yvonne said. "You gonna take one of the new rigs we got?"

Clem shook his head. "Nope. I kinda like living in the Dodge City Hotel. Reminds me of a vacation in Westworld."

Sid chuckled. "Oh, really? Got any robot dance hall girls, I wonder?"

"Stop," Yvonne said. "You've been spending a lot of time with Sarah, Clem."

"Nothing romantic about that. We're old friends, that's all."

"You just do whatever makes you happy," Yvonne said. She turned to Sid. "Let's go, honey."

He nodded, and they walked down a couple more blocks, to where there were widely-spaced rows of battle wagons, most already in siege mode, lights on in about half of them.

"I think Sarah wants to be more than just friends," Yvonne whispered when they got out of earshot.

"I doubt it, frankly," Sid said. "He's older, you know. By more than a few years. He's had problems, too."

"Problems?"

"The usual older man problems," Sid said. "Do I have to spell it out for you?"

"You look nervous mentioning that. Worried? You still do fine."

"I do, but I'm not looking forward to the time that I won't anymore," he said. "Clem's twelve years older than me."

"That just puts him at seventy-five," she said. "Not that old. I actually thought he was older."

Sid unlocked the coach and opened the door for Yvonne. After he followed, she turned and hugged him, giving him a kiss which grew passionate.

"Wow, maybe I ought to stay here," he said.

"No, go and find out what you can, but just remember that I'll be here waiting."

Sid laughed. "You don't want me to drink too much."

"Yep, and I don't want you to be out too late either. Might as well use the tools I've been given."

"Oh, brother," Sid said. "I'm being worked."

She kissed him again, then whispered in his ear. "I want you. Be ready."

He smiled as she broke the embrace and walked to the fridge, looking inside.

"You're something," he said, shaking his head. "I'll be back sooner than you expect."

She waved, and he walked out the door. The evening was cooling down fast, Sid taking his time as he strolled back to Main Street. He could hear people. The population of the town had already swelled by a few hundred, most of the newcomers camped in tents to the east. The voices grew louder as he made it to the wooden sidewalk. Light flooded out of the saloon and the lobby of the hotel. Sid pushed through the swinging doors of the saloon. Clem was at the bar with Ed, Sam, and Garrett, Willard behind the bar.

"There he is," Clem said, smiling as Sid sat on the stool next to him.

"What'll you have?" Willard asked. "Some of that good stuff?"

"Sure, on the rocks," Sid said, putting his elbows on the bar. He turned to look at the room, all the tables full. Seth and Kaitlyn were in the back, at the same table as always, staring into the laptop screen, Trevor and Kaylee sitting next to them.

"Jumpin place," Clem said, taking a sip of his whiskey. Willard slid Sid's to him.

"Thanks," Sid said, putting the glass to his lips. "Damn fine liquor."

"We're flush, after that last bit that Elmer and I found," Willard said. "It don't come out for everybody."

Garrett laughed. "I'd put it away if my crazy sister shows up."

"I saw Elmer go over there half an hour ago," Willard said. "She's either down for the night, or she'll stomp over here shortly, ready for a squall."

Ed laughed, shaking his head. "And I thought the tribe was a soap opera."

"Mine was," Sid said. "Where's Ji-Ho?"

"He wasn't feeling well," Sam said. "Hit the sack. I think he wants to be fresh when his friends arrive."

"When are they due?" Sid asked.

"Couple hours, if they don't run into problems."

"They're coming all the way from Sacramento in one day, with the roads how they are now?"

"The roads aren't bad further north," Sam said. "Things have settled down nicely thanks to Ivan's efforts up there."

"And thanks to the citizens, let's not forget," Clem said. "Californians have exceeded my expectations."

"True that," Sid said. "Where's Sarah?"

"Stop that," Clem said, smiling. "There's nothing there. Really. Besides, she's still mourning. John hasn't been gone for that long."

"I miss that man so much," Sam said, raising his glass. "Here's to him."

The others joined the toast.

"Clem told you guys what happened out there, right?" Sid asked.

"Yep," Sam said.

"Sorry about your men," Sid said to Garrett.

"Thanks," he said. "That was tough. Wish we had a better way to track them. Maybe those cameras will help."

"There's a bunch of armed off-roaders coming with Jules," Sam said. "We ought to enlist them to join the patrols."

"How safe do you guys think we are here?" Sid asked.

"We're getting thousands more people, and a lot of them have military weapons," Garrett said. "It'll be an armed camp. I don't think the enemy will continue to hit us. We'll kill too many of them."

"The enemy forces in Mexico are moving north again," Seth said in a loud voice. "I think it's because those forces from the south are almost with them."

"Dammit, I knew that's why they were waiting," Sam said. "Thanks, Seth."

"No problem. We're gonna hit the rack pretty soon. Want me to leave the laptop?"

"Nah, all of us have phones," Sam said.

"Okay," Seth said, unplugging his power supply. He got ready to leave with Kaitlyn, Trevor, and Kaylee.

"Seth's a lucky kid," Clem said. "His woman is a looker."

"You got that right," Willard said. "Makes me wish I was about sixty years younger."

The men laughed.

"You guys hear any more about the forces in San Diego?" Sid asked. "The air support?"

Clem chuckled. "You're here to find out the latest, then you're going back home, aren't you? Yvonne wants to get a report, I'll bet."

Sid snickered. "How'd you guess? We're both interested."

"I tried to talk Anna into coming over, but she decided to hang out at the ranch house instead," Garrett said.

Sam smiled. "Erica wanted to stay at home with Mia, but she wants info too. We're all in the same boat."

Clem laughed. "Good reason to be single. I'll have another drink, bar keep. Should I open a tab?"

"You guys can drink for free," Willard said. "In fact, everybody can drink for free, as far as I'm concerned."

Garrett eyed him. "I don't want no drunken brawls in town, though, okay Willard? Take it easy with folks we don't know."

"Of course," Willard said, sliding a fresh drink to Clem.

"Thank you kindly," Clem said, a twinkle in his eye.

"In the morning we should go follow the tracks, and figure out where those UN Peacekeepers came in," Sid said.

"I second that," Garrett said. "Hell, I'll probably go with you if Anna doesn't have plans for me."

"Plans?" Sam asked.

Ed chuckled. "Moving right in, is she?"

Garrett shrugged. "She's the woman of the house already. What can I say. I wanted it."

"What time tomorrow?" Sid asked, downing his drink.

"Not too early," Garrett said. "I'm gonna drink a tad more. Things are gonna get way too busy around here when we get the large influx of recruits."

"Sounds like you're thinking more than a tad," Willard said. "Think I'll join you."

"Yeah, until Susanne shows up," Clem said.

"She can only pull that crap with Elmer," Willard said.

"That's a true statement," Garrett said. "I love my sister and all, but I don't understand how he can put up with that."

"You probably don't want to know," Clem quipped. The others cracked up.

"Yeah, I guess you're right about that," Garrett said.

"How about nine, Garrett?" Sid asked, getting off the stool.

"Nine thirty, okay?"

"Done," Sid said. "See you guys in the morning."

Sid left the bar, heading back out onto the wooden sidewalk, re-tracing his steps. He caught Sarah out of the corner of his eye. She rushed across the street from the boarding house.

"Clem in the saloon?" she asked.

"Yeah," Sid said, stopping on the sidewalk, leaning against a hitching post. "Why? Problems?"

"I heard he almost got killed today," she said.

"Now where'd you hear a thing like that?" Sid asked.

"Garrett told Susanne. Clem is too smart to lose. Was he doing something stupid?"

"No more than the rest of us," Sid said. "Hell, Yvonne helped us a lot. Killed two of the snipers. Clem did well out there, too. He got those cameras placed. They'll give us at least some view of that area."

"I don't think you guys should be taking him out there," she said softly.

"He's younger than he looks, you know."

"How old *is* he?"

"He's never told you that?" Sid asked.

"I know he's older than you and John."

"He's only seventy-five," Sid said.

"Really? I thought he was in his eighties."

"I'll tell him you said that," Sid said with a wicked grin.

"Don't you dare. He's still in there, huh?"

"Garrett, Clem, Ed, and Willard are gonna drink a little more. It'll be too crazy to do that after all the additional people show up."

"Thanks," she said, turning towards the saloon.

"Where are you going?"

"Maybe I'd like a few drinks too," she said. "Go home to Yvonne."

Sid chuckled, and headed back to the coach. It was dark, except for the reading light in the bedroom.

"Sid?" Yvonne called from the back.

"It's me," he said, shuffling along in the dark. He bumped into the kitchen counter.

"Turn on a light, silly."

"I'm coming straight there," he said, walking to the back. She was under the covers with a book in her hand.

"Well, what do you have to report?"

"Lots more people arriving tomorrow. Sam and Ji-Ho's buddies should be here later tonight."

"They're driving straight through?"

"Apparently," he said, pulling off his shirt. "We're going back out to follow the trails of the UN Peacekeepers tomorrow morning."

"Who's we?"

"Garrett's interested. Not sure who else."

"I'm going," she said. "What else?"

"Seth said that the lower group of enemy fighters has caught up with the big group, and they started moving again."

"Oh, God," she said. "That all?"

Sid pulled off his pants and climbed into bed, laying on his back. "Yeah, that's pretty much it. We teased Clem a little bit about Sarah, and teased Garrett a little bit about Anna."

"It's not nice to tease," Yvonne said, rolling over the top of him and settling in.

"You're naked."

"So are you, I've noticed," Yvonne said, kissing him gently. "I like it." Their hands roamed on each other, the conversation slowing. Then Sid laughed.

"What?" Yvonne asked, stopping her movement for a moment.

"Sarah met me on the sidewalk while I was on my way here."

"Oh, really," Yvonne asked, looking him in the eyes. "Why?"

"She wanted to know where Clem was. Susanne told her what happened."

Yvonne snickered, then went back to kissing Sid, on his mouth, then on his neck and chest. He was kissing her back now, focused on the nape of her neck.

"I'm liking this," he whispered.

"Did she go home?" Yvonne asked, moving her head closer to his.

"Who?"

"Duh," she said.

"Oh, Sarah. You're not helping my concentration."

"So deal with it," she said. "Tell me."

He sighed. "She went to the saloon, said she was gonna drink with the others."

Yvonne stopped, backing up to see his face. "No way."

"I'm serious," he said. "Get back down here."

"You know what she wants, don't you?" Yvonne whispered.

"She wants to tell him to be more careful, I expect."

She shook her head, getting up higher, then sinking herself onto him, moaning. "She wants this." Sid watched as she shuddered over him, moving faster, already out of control, crying out as the passion took them over.

***

The bobtail truck and several vans were lined up on the dark street in an industrial area, just south of Sacramento. A handful of college-aged men and women were loading the back with computer and audio equipment. Ben Dover walked out the door of the rented office suite, which stood between two larger spaces for manufacturing and storage.

"That everything?" Ben Dover asked, looking in the back of the truck at the equipment packed inside.

"Yes sir," said a young man with dark shaggy hair and an olive complexion, having the look of a TV star. "Are we leaving now?"

"Yep," Ben said.

"Where are we going?"

"I can't say," Ben said. "We can never stay in the same place for long. This is just routine. You know that."

"So, we aren't going to the southern base, then?"

Ben eyed him. "What's your name again?"

"Eric," he said. "Just joined you last week."

"Uh huh," Ben said. "You ask too many questions."

He looked embarrassed. "Sorry. I'm still feeling my way around with this organization."

"How did you find out about us?"

The young man shot him a worried glance. "Friend of Ivan's."

"What's his name?" Ben asked, thinking about where his gun was.

The young man didn't answer right away.

"I'm waiting," Ben said.

"I can't remember his name. It's on the tip of my tongue. It's one of those Russian names. Somebody who knew him in grade school, back in the old country."

"Okay, never mind," Ben said, walking away. When he was out of sight he sent a text to Ivan, telling him about the exchange.

"Oh, there you are," Eric said, coming around the back of the truck. "Which vehicle do you want me in?"

"Third one from the back," Ben said as his phone dinged with the text return. After Eric walked away, he looked at it. *Kill him now.*

Ben's heart was in his throat. He'd killed since this started, more than once, but it always got to him.

"Hey, Eric," Ben yelled. "Forgot about something. I need your help. Come over here."

Sean, one of Ben's other people, had watched what was going on. He got close to Ben and whispered. "I've got your back. Don't trust this one."

"Get by the door of the suite," Ben whispered. Eric was back, trying to force a smile on his face as he approached.

"C'mon," Ben said. "We're going into the back-office. We need to dismantle the desk in there and take it. We're short on those where we're going."

"Oh, that was what the text was about?"

"Text?" Ben asked, following the young man into the office suite.

"I heard one come to your phone."

"Oh," Ben said. "Yes."

They got to the back office, Ben closing the door behind them. He pulled his weapon. Eric whirled around, his eyes getting big. His hand went behind his back.

"Freeze or I'll shoot," Ben said in a loud voice, knowing that Sean would hear it.

Eric raised his hands above his head. "Don't shoot."

The door opened, Sean rushing in with his pistol in a two-handed combat grip.

"He's got a gun in his back waistband. Get it. I'll cover."

"My pleasure," Sean said, reaching around and pulling the small pistol out. He stuck it into his pocket, then frisked Eric. "Clean."

"Who are you working for?" Ben asked.

"I can't say," Eric said, trembling. "They'll kill me."

"If you don't say, I'll kill you," Ben said. "Make your choice."

"How did you know?"

"You think Ivan grew up in Russia," Ben said. "You weren't prepared well by whoever sent you."

Sean laughed, then got a serious expression on his face. "He might have friends around."

"All they wanted me to do was tell them where you went," Eric said.

"Yeah, so they could come kill us," Sean said.

Ben shook his head. "They probably think we're going to the same place Ivan is going. Like we'd do that."

"Can you just let me go?" Eric asked. "Please? I won't tell anybody."

Ben ignored him, turning to Sean. "Get the others on all of our vehicles with the bug detectors."

Sean nodded yes and left the office.

"Who are you working for?" Ben asked again.

"The UN," he said softly.

Ben sighed. "I already knew that. If it were anybody else, you'd have an RFID chip. Who specifically are you working for?"

Gunfire erupted outside. Eric lost it, crying now, begging for his life.

"You have a frigging wire on or something," Ben said, pointing the gun at his head and firing. He poked his head out of the office, watching as his small team was killed by a group of UN commandos. "Dammit." Grabbing his gun, he bolted towards the back of the facility, slipping out the door and running into the shadows. The sound of gunfire went on for another minute or two. Then he pulled out his cellphone, loading the demolition app. He pushed the button, and a large explosion went off, pieces of bob-tail truck flying high enough into the air to be seen from behind the building. A quick text to Ivan, and then he disappeared into the night.

{11}

Pool Pickup

Ben ran out of the dark industrial area, heart pounding. His whole team, gone in an instant. He had to contact Ivan, but was afraid to stop. Sirens approached, probably coming to check out the gunfire and the burning truck. He ran towards the opening in back, which went into a vacant lot, hiding in trees about fifty yards out, then hit Ivan's contact on his phone and put it to his ear.

"Ben, you left yet?" Ivan asked.

"They're gone," he said, trying to catch his breath. "All of them."

"What happened?" Ivan asked.

"The plant tipped off the enemy," he said. "I was questioning him in the office when UN commandos attacked the group outside."

"Did they get the computers?" Ivan asked.

"I used the self-destruct. I'll never doubt you again about that kind of thing. Sorry."

"Don't be sorry," Ivan said. "You're learning faster than anyone I've ever had on my team. You sure everybody's dead?"

"Pretty sure. Nobody was returning fire before I blew the truck. Somebody might have survived, but now I hear sirens approaching. Want me to go back and check?"

"NO!" Ivan said. "Get away from there, find a good place to get picked up, and I'll send Mr. White and Mr. Black. They're nearby. Got it?"

"Yeah," Ben said. "We were lucky. Can't believe this jerk thought you were from Russia."

"Morons," Ivan said. "Protect yourself. We need you to rebuild the team. That recruitment is essential, with the forces we've got coming at us now."

"I've got my phone, and we're rolling big time with the recruitment. I think we did enough before we packed up. These campaigns develop a life of their own once they get going."

"Good," Ivan said. "We'll get you on a plane to the south. I'll have new facilities ready to go. Don't get killed. Call me when you're in a place you can be picked up."

"I'll do my best," Ben said. He ended the call and crept further back in the vacant lot, heading for a housing tract that backed up to it, climbing a fence into a back yard and rushing for the front gate, the dog next door barking. He burst out of it just as lights came on in the house, his heart hammering in his chest, running full speed down the sidewalk towards a park at the end, getting into the shadows before anybody got outside. There was play equipment there, in an area with a rubber floor. He slipped into a play fort, hidden from the outside, and watched for a few minutes. The only sound was the sirens, and then the thumping of a chopper. *Dammit.*

The chopper came into view over the industrial area, circling, it's spotlight shining, making a beam in the damp night air. The lights in the house he just ran past were on now, a man standing on the front lawn looking around, his cellphone to his ear. "He's calling the police," Ben whispered to himself, looking around for a better hiding place. The community pool was sixty yards away, with a club house and cabanas, sitting dark and un-occupied. *Run.*

He slipped away from the play equipment, not running until he was out of sight of the man, who was still looking around, phone to his ear. The ground between him and the pool complex seemed like a mile, but he crossed it in seconds, climbing the fence and getting into the shadows, under a patio roof with a towel cabinet and a row of lounge chairs. The pool was dark, wind putting gentle ripples on the surface, the large round spa also dark. Chlorine smell. There was a click, and the pump started, the flow of water in the pool barely audible.

The sound of a car approached, a K-9 unit driving slowly up the street towards the house. He could hear car doors opening and closing, the police chopper going in wider circles now. On the edge of panic, he texted Ivan.

"I'm hiding at a pool, in the housing track past lot behind office. K-9 unit and choppers approaching."

An officer was walking towards the park, holding the leash of a big dog. The text ding startled him, and he frantically shut the ringer off and read, trying to block the light of the screen with his hands.

"In area, diversion in seconds, be ready, black sedan."

Suddenly there was a huge explosion at their former office, a massive fireball rising. The officer ran back to his vehicle, pulling the dog, who was looking back at Ben most of the way. The chopper moved towards the blast, the police cruiser racing out of the tract, siren going on as they got to the main street. A few seconds later the black sedan pulled up. Ben got up, jumped the fence, and ran, getting into the back seat.

"Put on seat belt," Mr. Black said, smiling back at him from the driver's seat.

"Ben Dover, good to see," Mr. White said as the car peeled out, heading out of the tract, going the opposite direction of the melee.

"How'd you guys get here so fast?" Ben asked, trying to catch his breath.

"Boss dispatched right away," Mr. White said. "He know where office is, you know."

"Oh, yeah," Ben said. "Where are we going?"

"Franklin Field," Mr. Black said as he turned onto the southbound I-5 onramp.

"Laptop on seat for you," Mr. White said. "Work recruitment. Time short. Chartered plane pick up."

"You guys going too?" Ben asked.

"No, boss leave us here to watch state government, make sure no slippage," Mr. Black said.

***

Sarah slowed as she approached the saloon, heart beating a little faster than she liked. There was laughter coming from inside. The doors swung open, one almost smacking her as two people came out.

"Oh, sorry," said one of them, tipping his cowboy hat.

"It's okay," Sarah said, feeling her face flush. She pushed through the swinging doors. The room was starting to empty out, only the bar fully occupied. Willard saw her come in and smiled broadly.

"Howdy," he said. "Want a drink? I'm buying."

"Sarah," Sam said, seeing her walk in. Ed and Garrett turned, nodding a greeting, Clem seeing her and smiling.

"This taken?" she asked, standing by the stool next to Clem.

"It is now," Clem said, eyes light with booze, voice still clear as a bell.

"Want some of the good stuff?" Willard asked.

"What's the *good stuff?*" she asked.

"Whiskey from the folks who mined here," Garrett said. "It's probably about a hundred years old."

"Really?" she asked, settling onto the stool, her elbows going onto the bar. "This place isn't that old, is it?"

"The saloon?" Willard asked. "Nah, we built this about eight years ago. The mine is another story, and there was a basement under the ruins we build on. Original bar sat here, I reckon."

"We know it did," Garrett said. "Surprised the place ain't haunted."

"Maybe it is," Ed said, grinning at the others. "This is damn fine whiskey, but I think I'd better slow down."

"You got to drive anyplace?" Clem asked.

Ed chuckled. "No, I guess not."

"I'll try some of the good stuff," Sarah said demurely.

"On the rocks, or mixed with soda, or a shot?" Willard asked.

"Give me a shot," she said. The others chuckled as Willard grabbed a shot glass from under the bar and picked up the ancient unlabeled bottle. He poured carefully and slid it over to her.

"It might be a little harsh," Clem said, watching as she picked it up.

She smiled at him and then tossed it back, her body shuddering as it burned its way down. "Wow."

"Told you," Clem said. "I like it on the rocks. That way I can sip and enjoy the flavor."

"I never liked the whiskey taste much," she said, setting the shot glass down. "Wow, you feel this fast, right behind the forehead."

"Another?" Willard asked.

"Oh, what the hell," she said. He refilled her glass, the others watching.

"You drink much?" Garrett asked.

"Rarely," she said, looking down at the shot glass. "John had a problem, and I didn't want to encourage it, so I drank a lot less in the last fifteen years than I did in my youth." She tossed the drink down, shuddering a little less than the first time, the light feeling in her head growing. "This is nice. I do like to drink. Usually something a little weaker, though."

"We've got a full bar," Willard said, "I don't know much about those sweet drinks that women like, though. I'm more of a pourer than a mixer. We've got some white wine if you're interested."

"Never mix the grain with the grapes," Sam quipped.

"I think that comment was meant for beer, not whiskey," Garrett said.

"What's whiskey made of?" Sarah asked, pushing her shot glass towards Willard.

"You sure, honey?" Willard asked.

She nodded yes, so he poured.

"Whiskey is made from corn," Sam said. "That's a grain, isn't it?"

"Kinda sorta," Ed said. "*Corn squeezens.*"

Garrett laughed. "Isn't that what Granny Clampett called it?"

Sarah giggled. "Rheumatiz medicine."

"Oh, yeah," Clem said. "Loved that show."

"Grits and gopher jowls," Ed said, laughing. "Hell, I need another drink."

"I'd better get back," Sam said. "Erica's gonna wonder what happened to me."

"Text her," Garrett said.

"Yeah, she'll understand," Ed said. "Have some fun with the boys."

"Hey," Sarah said. She laughed, then drank the next shot, not shuddering at all this time, savoring the warm feeling as it went down her throat. "I'm kinda liking this."

"You're gonna start slurring in a second, if you're not careful," Clem said. "This stuff hits women harder than it hits men."

"That's a fact," Willard said.

"I've only had three," she said.

"Well, I've had five, and I'm pretty tight," Willard said. "Probably have more, though."

There was yelling across the street. Willard and Garrett looked at each other and cracked up.

"What's going on?" Sam asked.

"Elmer and Susanne again," Willard said.

"He's going to end up here, I suspect," Clem said.

"Nah, they'll just stay there and fight for a while," Garrett said.

"Nothing violent, I hope," Sarah said.

"Never," Garrett said. "That's why I told Clem to stay at the hotel instead of her boarding house."

"Maybe you should've warned me too," Sarah quipped.

"You already moved in before I had the chance," Garrett said. "Don't worry, they don't do it every night."

"It's been fine until now," Sarah said, sliding her shot glass back to Willard.

"You're gonna be feeling no pain, you know," Willard said as he poured.

"Good," she said. "I could use a break. Letting loose a little isn't bad every once in a while. It's good for you, actually." The last of the sentence was a little slurred. Willard eyed Clem, smiling. He shook his head.

"What?" Sarah asked.

"Nothing," Willard said. "Bar etiquette."

"What's bar etiquette?" she asked.

"It's where the bartender makes sure there's somebody with a person to help them home."

"Message received," Clem said, "but who's gonna help me home?"

Everybody laughed.

"I'm okay," Sarah said. "Not like I have to get into the car and drive."

"Yeah, you only have to cross a muddy, rutted street and brave three flights of stairs," Garrett said.

"It's not muddy," Clem said.

"Just trying to be colorful," Garrett said, smiling at him.

"How are you getting home, Garrett?" Sam asked. "Your place is a lot further."

Garrett smiled. "Anna. She'll come get me in the wagon."

"She knows how to drive a team of horses?" Sarah asked.

Ed laughed. "Oh, yeah, she's got that down."

"She does," Garrett said, "but this is just a carriage with one horse. She'll probably be here soon. Maybe I can talk her into a drink or two."

"That won't be too difficult," Ed said. "Trust me on that."

More shouting drifted across the street.

"Geez," Sarah said.

"Decent squall," Willard said.

"Yeah, I was gonna say," Sam said. "Hit me again." He pushed his glass to Willard, who filled it with ice and whiskey.

"Maybe I ought to do it that way," Sarah said.

"It'll slow you down a tad," Clem said. "Not a bad thing. I'm enjoying the company."

She touched his arm, looking into his eyes for a long moment. "You're so nice to me."

"Oh, you know," he said. "Old friends."

"Yes, old friends," she said. "Can I have one on the rocks, Willard?"

"Of course," he said, fixing her one.

She took a sip of the cold whiskey, savoring it for a moment. "You know, this isn't bad."

"I'll take another of those," Clem said.

"Me too, Willard said, filling both glasses with ice and pouring.

"There they go again," Sarah said as the voices drifted across the street. She looked at Clem and laughed. "Hope it's worth it to them."

"If they stop and Elmer doesn't end up over here, it's worth it," Willard said.

Garrett laughed. "Hey, that's my sister you're talking about."

"Elmer needs more protection than she does," Willard said.

"That sounded kinda naughty," Sarah said, slurring a little more.

Willard chuckled. "Actually, I'm kinda envious. Not of Susanne, mind you, but of the situation."

Sam's phone rang. "Uh oh, maybe I stayed too late." He looked at it. "Ji-Ho." He got off his stool and walked away, having a hushed conversation.

"Crap, I hope the party isn't over," Clem said. "I'm enjoying this."

"Me too," Sarah said.

Sam came back with a wide grin on his face. "We're about to have company."

"They're here?" Garrett asked.

"Yep, just pulling in now," Sam said. He typed out a text and sent it.

"What now?" Ed asked him.

"I just let Erica know not to wait up. I haven't seen these guys for a while."

"Maybe I'd better go into the basement and grab a few more bottles of the good stuff," Willard said.

Garrett nodded. "Yeah, do that."

"How are you doing?" Clem asked Sarah.

"Fine. Glad I slowed down a little. I was on the edge of control there for a while. Feeling better now."

"Good," Clem said.

The swinging doors creaked, everybody turning to see Ji-Ho coming in, followed by Ted, Jules, Tex, and Sparky.

"Why are you always in a saloon, you old son of a bitch?" Ted asked, walking up to Sam. They embraced.

"Been way too long," Sam said. "Tex, how the hell are you?"

"Never been better, partner. This looks like my kind of place."

"Hey, Sam," Sparky said. "Long time no see. You remember Jules?"

"Sure," Sam said. "How's it going, Jules?"

"Very good, old friend. Great to finally be with you."

Sam and Ji-Ho introduced everybody, while Willard lined up drinks for all.

"You okay, Ji-Ho?" Sam asked, eyeing him.

"Tired," he said softly. "Illness is progressing a little, but I'll be okay tomorrow if I get enough sleep. I leave soon."

"We have development tonight, need to discuss for minute," Jules said. "Mind?"

"No problem here," Garrett said. "Maybe we ought to go sit at the round table over there. Easier to chat."

"Yeah, do that, and I'll bring a bottle over," Willard said.

"That stuff is insane," Tex said. "What kind is it?"

Willard told him as they walked over, holding the bottle up in front of him.

"Damn, this stuff is over a hundred years old?" Tex asked. "No wonder it's so good."

"You need me?" Clem asked.

"Not unless you're interested," Sam said. "I'll fill you in later."

"Great, thanks," Clem said. Sarah looked at him and mouthed *thank you.*

"I hear from Ivan little while ago," Jules said. "Ben Dover's recruitment team got attacked when they were moving out of their offices in Sacramento."

"No," Ji-Ho said. "Did anybody survive?"

"Ben only," Jules said. "He already picked up, getting on plane tonight. He come here, set up, if that okay."

"Fine by me," Garrett said, "but what about our situation? Wasn't he the key to fielding a million citizens?"

"Yes," Jules said, "luckily they got beyond hump, recruitment snowballing. We should be good, but he need to develop new team. Maybe you have people who can help. Your data man, no?"

"Seth," Sam said. "Yeah, he'd be helpful, I'm sure, and his history program is running now. He's got his woman helping him, and she's very sharp. She can keep that going by herself while he works with Ben Dover."

"Anything more?" Ji-Ho asked.

"That was the main thing," Ted said. "You look way too tired. Go to bed. We'll catch up in the morning."

"Thanks," Ji-Ho said. "Glad you all here. Great to see. Good night." He got up and walked out the door.

"He's in bad shape, partner," Tex said.

"I'm with him every day, so I'm not seeing it as sharply as you are," Sam said. "Hope he can hold it together."

"Does the team know about his cancer?" Ted asked.

"Only a few of us," Sam said. "He doesn't want his niece to know, but it's gonna come to a head pretty soon, I'm afraid."

"Is Ivan really coming here?" Garrett asked.

Jules chuckled. "He'll make an appearance, I'm sure, but he like ghost. All over the place. Hard to pin down. Hard to keep track."

"I'd like to meet him," Ed said. "Love his style."

"He does have that," Ted said. "He's a little more docile than he used to be, from what I can tell."

"Oh, I don't know, partner," Tex said. "The enemy might not agree."

"That good point," Jules said, a wicked grin on his face. "Well, I go. Have lovely woman waiting. See in morning."

"Same here," Tex said. "I'll walk with you. Thanks for the fine whiskey, Willard."

"It's an honor to serve," Willard said. "I'm sure we'll toss a few back in the coming days."

"I'll stick around for a little while, I think," Sparky said.

"Me too, if you don't mind," Ted said.

"Okay, guys, have fun," Tex said, walking out with Jules.

"Another drink?" Willard asked the remaining men.

"I'm game," Ted said.

The others nodded in agreement, so Willard poured.

Boxcars

Clem and Sarah watched as Jules and Tex left the saloon. The argument across the street flared up again, Willard and Garrett laughing, telling the others about the situation.

"Sam is so glad to see those guys," Clem said.

"You know anything about them?"

"War buddies, basically." Clem got up and went behind the bar, getting some ice for his glass. "You want another?"

"Don't know if I should," she said. "Oh, what the heck." She drank down the last few drops and slid the glass to him. He made the new drinks, shooting a glance at Willard, who gave him a thumb up.

"I can't believe Susanne and Elmer," Sarah whispered as Clem sat next to her again, leaning in close.

"Hard way to live," Clem said, "but then you don't know what's between a couple. The make-up sex might be a big part of their dynamic."

Sarah blushed. "That's what they were talking about, huh?"

"Did I really just say that?" Clem asked.

She touched his shoulder. "It's okay. We're both adults, you know."

"I guess," Clem said, taking a sip. "This stuff has me going pretty good."

"I'm drunk. Been a lot of years."

"You aren't slurring as much," Clem said.

She giggled. "You're slurring more. I think it's kinda cute. You never drank that much back at the RV Park."

"Oh, I drank quite a bit," Clem said, "but up to a certain point, I hide it well."

"You're beyond that point tonight," Sarah said, shooting him a grin.

"Maybe a tad."

"How much is a tad?" she asked, her eyes dancing with his.

"More than a smidgen, I guess."

She punched him playfully on the upper arm. "That's not an answer."

"Sure it is," he said. "Maybe not a *good* answer."

She laughed, then took another sip of her drink. "My head feels tingly."

"I'm sure it does. Mine does. I like it." He smiled, turning to look at the table, where the others were chatting and laughing. "They're having fun."

"You want to join them?" Sarah asked.

"No, I'm having a better time with you. We can if you want to, though."

The doors creaked, swinging as Anna walked in.

"Uh oh," Sarah whispered. "The jig's up."

Clem snickered.

"Garrett, you ready to go?" Anna asked.

"Everybody, this is Anna," Garrett said. "The woman of the house."

She smiled, shaking her head. "How much have you had to drink?"

"Quite a bit," Garrett said. "Come join us."

She sighed, then came over. "Where am I gonna sit?" Garrett pushed back and patted his lap.

"Not in this lifetime," she said, pulling a chair next to his. She sat down, and Garrett introduced her to the others.

"Well that was interesting," Clem said. "At least she doesn't look mad."

"She's totally infatuated with Garrett," Sarah whispered. "Look at them. That's nice."

"It is," Clem said, moving closer to her. Then the arguing across the street started again, and he laughed.

"They haven't gotten to the fun part yet, I guess," Sarah said.

Clem looked at her, studying her eyes, quiet for a moment, then snapping out of it and looking away. He took another sip of whiskey.

"Mine's almost out already," Sarah said.

"Another?"

"Not so sure that would be a good idea," she said, "you having another?"

"I'm thinking about it. I'd like to, but I'd probably regret it."

"Then don't," she said. "I think I've had enough."

"Anna's taking Garrett home," Clem said, watching the couple get up and say their goodbyes. They went out the door, the sound of horse hoofs starting, fading away as they headed down the street.

"Maybe I should be going too," Sarah said.

"I'll walk you home."

"That would be nice," she said, getting off the stool. Clem did the same. They were part way to the door when the arguing started again.

"Geez," Clem said.

"Hey, there's open rooms in the hotel, if you want to stay there instead of the peanut gallery across the street," Willard said.

Sarah thought about it for a moment. "All my stuff is at the boarding house."

"Whatever you want to do," Willard said. "The keys for the empty rooms are hanging on the wall behind the front desk."

"Who's watching that?" Clem asked.

Willard chuckled. "Me."

Ted, Sparky, and Sam cracked up.

"Remind me not to leave you in charge," Sam said. "Just kidding."

"I'll walk you to the boarding house to get your stuff, then back to the hotel if you'd like," Clem said.

She looked at him. "That's too much bother."

"No it's not, and the night air will do both of us some good."

"All right." They went out the doors, walking down the wooden sidewalk, then crossing the dusty street, entering the front door of the boarding house. "You can wait down here. No need for two of us to go up all those stairs."

"Are you sure you're okay?" Clem asked.

"I feel quite a bit better already," she said, trying to ignore the angry words as she got to the stairwell.

Clem sat on a couch in the parlor, looking around at the replica décor Susanne had used. The yelling finally stopped, Clem wondering if Sarah wouldn't just stay there instead. She came down the stairs a couple minutes later with a bag in her hand, her face red.

"What happened?" he asked.

"They're into the fun part now," she whispered. "I heard more than I wanted to."

"Oh," Clem said, laughing. "You can stay here if you want, then."

"No, that will bother me as much as the yelling, I suspect, especially now."

"Why especially now?"

"Because of the drinking," she said, smiling as they walked out the door.

"Feels nice out here," Clem said.

"Very nice. At least it's helping the flush on my face."

They strolled across the street and onto the wood sidewalk, going past the saloon.

"Looks like the rest of them are calling it a night," Clem said.

"They've been on the road. They're probably beat."

"Probably." There was a dim light on in the lobby of the hotel. Clem opened the door for Sarah, and followed her to the front desk. The wall behind had mail cubby holes and hooks, about half of which had keys.

"Which one are you in again?" she asked.

"Room twelve," he said. "Nice view of the street."

"Room eleven is open," she said. "I'll take that one. Still makes me a little nervous being alone, you know."

"It hasn't been that long," Clem said. "Perfectly understandable."

She picked the key off the hook, and they headed for the stairs, climbing up next to each other.

"There aren't bathrooms inside the rooms, are there?"

Clem laughed. "No, this is old-school. Men's and women's rooms, with showers. Down at the end of the hallway, towards the back. They're not bad. Good pressure in the showers. Kinda nice after what we've been living with."

"Our rooms are adjoining, aren't they?"

"Mine is adjoining with one of them. Not sure if it's eleven or thirteen."

They got to the top of the stairs and headed down the hallway, getting to Clem's room first.

"Well, which is it adjoining?" she asked as he unlocked his door.

"Yours," he said. "Let's make sure it opens." He followed her down to her door and watched her unlock it.

"It's fine," she said, looking inside. "Would it bother you if we had the adjoining doors unlocked?"

"You look nervous," Clem said. "You gonna be okay?"

"I'm just used to sleeping close to somebody I know, that's all," she said.

"I don't have a problem. Might want to knock first before you come in, though. I don't have any PJs."

She giggled. "Oh my."

He started for her door.

"You can just use the inside door if you want," she said.

"Okay," he said, looking nervous.

She smiled, giving him a quick hug. "Thank you for being such a gentleman."

"Gentleman?" Clem asked. "Even with my off-color remarks?"

She smiled. "I was pretty drunk earlier. You could've talked me into almost anything."

He shrugged. "I could say the same thing, you know."

She looked at him funny, but then smiled. "Okay, good night." She kissed him on the cheek, and watched him open the door. Then he laughed.

"Shoot, I have to open the second door from my side. Been a while since I've been in one of these rooms, and my brain still isn't firing on all cylinders."

"Still feeling it some, huh?" she asked.

"We drank a lot. Don't you feel it anymore?"

"I'm still half drunk," she said, following him to the door. "See you in the morning."

Clem nodded and left. She could hear him open and close his door, and then he knocked on the inside door. "You still decent?"

"Kinda," she said. "Open it."

He unlatched the door and pushed it open. "There, we know everything's hunky-dory," Clem said, not looking at her.

"What's the matter?" she asked.

"You said you were only kinda decent," he said.

"I was talking about my mental state, silly." She laughed, walking towards him. "Maybe we should've drank some more."

"I'd better go to bed," Clem said, looking embarrassed. He slipped back through the door, leaving it ajar. Sarah stood staring at it, a sly smile on her face.

***

The early morning sun couldn't quite burn through the fog covering the border. Doug had been awake since about four. Jorge was still asleep, in the back of his pickup truck, parked on the north side of Old Highway 80. There were thousands of citizen warriors in the area now, digging in and waiting for the onslaught they knew would come. The waiting was the hardest part for Doug. The enemy had been sitting in the same place, moving only a couple miles towards them in the last several hours. Food and other supplies flowed into the town daily. The rumor was that friends of liberty from around the globe were paying for it all, but there were never names.

"Hey, man, they're moving," Jorge said, head poking up from his truck bed. You see that?"

"About time you woke up," Doug said. "I haven't looked for a while. It's like watching paint dry."

"Look at it, man."

Doug nodded, pulling his phone out and loading the long-range app, his eyes getting wider. "They're ten miles further than they were last time I checked."

"Look behind them," Jorge said, climbing out of the truck bed.

"Dammit," Doug said. "Is that the other two hundred thousand?"

Jorge was next to him now. "Looks like."

"We're gonna get nailed," Doug said. He shot Jorge a glance that was nervous but resolute. "This is where I make my stand."

Jorge smiled, shaking his head. "We'll fight our best, but when it's time to split, we need to go. We're worth more to the nation alive than dead. Don't ever forget that."

Doug nodded. "I know, but what's coming might not be something we can escape."

"I'm worried for the men who are on the first few rows of claymore mines."

"Yes, they're in the most danger," Doug said, "but our position behind the k-rails won't stand up to much. You know that, right?"

"I do," Jorge said. "Feel a little guilty that we're not in the first couple rows."

"We're not fast enough," Doug said.

"Yeah, getting old sucks."

"Good morning," Conrad said, walking to them. "They're on the move."

"We saw," Jorge said. "Still a long walk, though."

"Indeed," Conrad said, "and they walked about half the night. I expect them to stop for a little while. We're still looking at more than a day before they can get here."

"How's the recruitment going?"

"We've got nearly three hundred thousand here now," he said, "but the road is clogged, so they're slowing some. Both I-8 and Old Highway 80 are backed up to Boulder Oaks towards the west, and to Ocotillo to the east. We're weighing the possibility of having them leave their cars and walk in."

"Boulder Oaks is over twenty miles from here, you know," Doug said, "and if we do that, the backup will go even further. Our forces won't get here in time."

"What about Highway 94?" Jorge asked.

"They've got the pass about half-way cleared," Conrad said, "but it's going faster now. Time-wise they're about three-quarters of the way done, from what my sources are telling me."

"Look at the map," Doug said. "That will just make the traffic backup worse."

Jorge put the phone to his face, moving fingers around on the map. "Dude, you're right. It dumps right onto Old Highway 80, at a spot we know is already gridlocked."

"*It is* moving," Conrad said, "but it's moving too slow."

"I was right," Doug said. "We're going to die here, but I'm ready. It's where we make our stand. We'll cut the enemy forces way back, so the number will be more manageable for the forces further north."

"But the cars," Jorge said.

Doug looked at him like he was nuts.

"What are we gonna drive on?" Doug asked. "The roads will be clogged. We'll get stuck in traffic when the enemy comes over the border, and we'll get picked off easily. Better to stay and fight them than to run when we're gonna get killed anyway."

Jorge sat down, his eyes showing panic. "I didn't get it before."

Conrad looked at both men, the harsh realization showing on his face. "This is our Alamo. Why didn't I realize it before now?"

Doug chuckled. "Well, on the good side, they'll build a monument here. People will remember. It'll be a shrine."

Conrad smiled. "That's the best attitude we can have now."

Jorge nodded in agreement, his expression melting into peaceful acceptance. "I wish we could get the damn Navy to start bombing these guys in Mexico. That would bring them down to a reasonable number in a hurry. Hell, might even end it completely. There's no cover in that desert. The enemy are sitting ducks."

"The brass are playing the long game," Conrad said. "Why risk widening the war when they know we've got enough people to stop the invasion further north?"

"They should say to hell with it and attack Mexico anyway," Doug said. "Hell, we've got half the US Army in Mexico right now."

"Those forces are being driven by the coalition," Conrad said, "with our phony federal government. That's a globalist adventure. We should have every politician who agreed to that shot for treason."

Conrad's phone rang. He walked away with it to his ear.

"First time I've seen him scared, man," Jorge said.

"Yeah. There's got to be something we can do."

"We've got nothing to do but wait and think," Jorge said. "We've dug in as much as we can. Maybe we can come up with a plan."

"Listen? Hear that?" Doug asked.

Jorge stopped talking, then his expression changed. "Crap, man, that sounds like a train."

"That's what I'm thinking," Doug said. "You ever see trains on that track anymore?"

"Not for years," Jorge said. "That line goes below the Mexican border, then back up. All the problems got it shut down."

"Then we might have enemy here already," Doug said. They both ran off the road to the tracks. Jorge put his ear to the rail.

"Yeah, it's a train all right."

"Let's get our guns," Doug said, rushing back towards their spot on the road.

"Wait, it might be our side, you know," Jorge said, rushing after him. "It just dips into Mexico by TJ. The US Navy probably controls that whole area."

"Better safe than sorry," Doug said, picking up the M60 he'd been issued, loading the belt of ammo.

"Is that what I think it is?" Conrad asked, running over.

"Yeah, man, it's a train," Jorge said. "We'll be able to see it in a minute. You think it's our guys?"

"Nobody told me anything," Conrad said, "but that's not unusual."

Four engines came into view, the train starting to slow as it approached.

Conrad got a huge grin on his face. "That's ours. Look at the artillery on those flatbeds! That's American stuff. Looks brand new!"

The train continued past them, a long freighter with twelve flatbeds, two artillery pieces on each, and a long row of boxcars behind it. It chugged to a stop, and a Marine officer jumped out of the first engine, followed by a couple staffers. They trotted over to where Conrad was, men leaving their positions to look.

"Who's in charge here?" he asked in a loud voice.

Conrad stepped forward. "Nobody is officially," he said. "I've been coordinating."

"Name?"

"Conrad," he said.

"I'm Lieutenant Colonel Meyers. We'd like to place these artillery pieces, but we need to do it in a hurry. There's three more trains on the way."

"Tell us how we can help," Doug said.

"Yes, we'll all lend a hand," Jorge said.

The boxcar doors opened, Marines climbing out, filling the area towards the rear of the train, all of them with packs and weapons.

"Holy crap," Conrad said. "How many men per boxcar?"

"With equipment and supplies, about sixty per car," he said. "The other trains are all box cars – each have about 150."

"How many men on this train?" Doug asked.

"Just over five thousand," Meyers said. "I heard you've placed rows of claymore mines."

"Yes sir," Conrad said, "and we've done a considerable amount of digging in. Most of our men have top-shelf weapons now, too. M4s and M60s, plus RPGs and other nice toys. The number of enemy troops coming is a problem. You know that, right?"

"What's the number of citizens here so far?" Meyers asked.

"We're getting close to three hundred thousand, and there's a lot more coming in on I-8, but the road is pretty clogged now. It's slow going. Some of them won't beat the enemy here."

"These tracks cross I-8 to the east," Jorge said. "We've got people stopped there too. Maybe we can get a whole bunch of people to drive off the road and get onto the boxcars – then we could ferry them over here. That would free the road up for more cars, too."

"I like that idea," Meyers said. "Last time I looked at these new apps, the enemy was thirty miles away. We've got about a day, and there's more trains coming past these three. We'll have at least nine total. Well trained Marines. Top notch."

"We still won't have enough, though," Conrad said. "We're talking just under ten thousand men per train if you can hold sixty per boxcar. There's seven hundred thousand enemy fighters on the way."

"We'll soften them up a lot with this artillery," Meyers said.

"Yeah, but I'll bet we can't use them until the enemy crosses the border," Doug said, shaking his head.

Meyers smiled. "Yep, those were the orders from General Sessions."

"Dammit," Conrad said.

"That jackass left the country with some of the other traitors at the Pentagon," Meyers said. "I think they know they're about to get nailed. Screw them. We start shelling the enemy positions as soon as we can get these pieces off the flatbeds."

"Then let's get them off the flatbeds," Conrad said with a wide grin.

{13}

Southern Strategy

The artillery pieces were off the flatbeds now, arrayed in a long row along Old Highway 80. Most of the fog had burned off, the desert heating up quickly, even though it was still before 8:00 AM. The empty train pulled forward on the tracks, heading east, as the next huge train pulled up in its place, Marines flooding out of the boxcars. Lieutenant Colonel Meyers directed placement of the men, and had a large team setting up mortars further back from the lines.

"We're gonna pound the hell out of whoever survives the shelling, dude," Jorge said.

"The enemy hasn't budged yet this morning," Doug said, looking at the apps.

"They'll start moving soon," Meyers said, walking to them, Conrad and several Marines following him. "We'll be able to relieve everybody from claymore mine duty."

"How?" Doug asked.

"Remote switches," Meyers said. "You're getting an upgrade. They'll be touched off from that hill back there."

"Good," Jorge said. "Still want us on the k-rail here?"

"I suggest you dig in further back," Meyers said. "We'll put the Marines up front. They've trained for this."

Jorge and Doug looked at each other, startled as the train bumped forward, now empty, the next one rolling in right behind it.

"We've got so many men now," Jorge said. An ear-splitting boom went off, making him and Doug jump. Conrad chuckled, looking at Meyers, who was sporting a wide grin. He pulled some earplugs out of his pocket and put them in.

"You guys have these?" he asked.

"Nope," Conrad said.

"We brought a lot of them," Meyers said. "Go see the men at the table in front of my tent. Spread the word, okay?"

"Yes sir," Doug said. The three men headed past the road, onto a flat stretch of ground about forty yards behind the k-rail, as more artillery shots went off behind them.

"That's their wake-up call," Jorge said. He pulled his phone out and looked at the apps. "Damn, dude, they're scattering."

"Hopefully a lot of them are dying," Conrad said, turning to look at the southern horizon. "Look at the smoke. Maybe we hit some of their ammo."

They got their ear plugs, Conrad scanning for a good place to dig in.

"See a likely spot?" Doug asked.

"Look at that ridge, right behind the train tracks," Conrad said. "Set up over there, and tell all of your team. You know where they are?"

"All over," Jorge said. "I'll send them a broadcast text."

"That would be good," Conrad said. "See you guys in a while. I'm gonna go find my men. We'll probably be close to you guys. There's not going to be room up front for anybody but Marines."

All the big guns were firing now, a round going off every thirty seconds.

"You think they're going to keep coming?" Jorge asked. "They might flee back to the south."

"I doubt it. Look at the app."

Jorge refreshed his. "Yep, they're spreading out wide."

"That's what I'd do. I'll bet the first few rounds took out quite a few, because they were bunched together."

"Think the artillery is that accurate? We can't see them."

"We know exactly where they are, because of the apps," Doug said. "They probably had it dialed in with the first shot."

***

Clem woke in the Dodge City Hotel as the sun from the window hit his face, his head pounding from the hangover.

"Whoa, haven't had one of these for a while." He sat up in bed, noticing that the doors between his room and Sarah's were opened wide.

"Not feeling so good, huh?" Sarah asked from her room. "Me neither."

Clem chuckled. "It'll pass."

She appeared in the doorway, standing in her nightgown. His eyes locked onto her, her form shadowed through the thin white cloth, thanks to the sun in her room. He looked away quickly, and she giggled.

"Sorry," he said.

"Well at least I have *something* on," she said. "Left my robe at the boarding house. I don't mind, if you don't."

"I wouldn't say that I mind, exactly," he said, turning back towards her, then holding his head. "Ouch."

"We're quite a pair, aren't we," she said, walking towards his bed. "What time is it, anyway?"

Clem reached for the phone on his bedside table, careful to keep the covers well above his waist. "It's only 8:30. Maybe we should sleep some more."

She sat on the side of his bed, now the light of his own window revealing her. "I'll stay in bed for a while. Move over."

He looked at her, eyes questioning, face turning read.

"Oh, please," she said, lifting the covers before he could protest and slipping inside. "I miss this the most." She settled next to him.

"Sarah," he whispered.

"We don't have to do anything," she said, "and I won't look if you don't want me too."

He laughed nervously, then held his head again. "Geez. Every time I move my head."

"Glad I didn't drink as much as you did," she said. "I'm not feeling *that* bad. Want me to get you some aspirin? I've got some in my purse."

"Isn't that at the boarding house?"

"No, it was in the bag I brought over," she said, getting up, her eyes glancing under the covers. He noticed, and they locked eyes. "Sorry. I didn't see much."

Clem shrugged as she walked into her room, trying to keep his eyes off her, but losing the battle. She walked back in and he looked away again, raising a smirk on her face.

"Land sakes, I obviously don't mind if you look," she said, picking up a glass from the table next to his wash basin, filling it from the pitcher. She brought it over and handed him two aspirins. "This should help a little."

He nodded as he took them, then laid down. She got back into bed, laying lightly against him. "Can we sleep a while longer? I like to spoon."

"You sure that's a good idea?" Clem asked.

She turned her back to him. "C'mon."

"Okay," he said, his heart pounding.

"Feels like you're okay."

"It won't last," he said. "Hasn't for a while."

"Don't worry about that," she said. "I think I'll move from the boarding house into the next-door room, though, if you don't mind."

He chuckled. "I thought you'd want to move into *this* room, after this."

She turned to him, smiling. "You want all the questions from our friends?"

He sighed. "No, not really. They'll ask them anyway if you move over here."

"No, they won't. Everybody heard the fracas last night. Perfect excuse, if we're not in the same room. After we've retired for the night, we can do whatever we want, you know."

"Well, this does feel nice, anyway," Clem said. "As long as you don't expect too much."

"I understand," she said.

"My headache is almost gone."

"The aspirin."

"That's only part of it." He settled as she laid back on her side again. They drifted off to sleep.

***

Ji-Ho struggled to get out of bed. He checked his phone. Almost 10:00? *Dammit.*

There was a rap on the door. "Uncle, are you okay?"

"I fine," Ji-Ho said as loud as he could muster.

"I'm coming in," she said, opening the door. She walked to the bedroom and saw him. "What's wrong?"

"Nothing. I be okay after I wake up a bit."

"You need to be honest with me." She sat down on the end of the bed. "I'm not blind, you know. This is happening more often."

He looked at her, his eyes tearing up.

"Uncle," she said softly. "You're sick. What is it? Cancer?"

He sighed and shook his head yes, not looking at her.

"You act as if that's something to be ashamed about."

"I hide from you," he said.

"You probably had your reasons. Does my auntie know?"

He nodded yes.

"How long do you have?"

"Doctor say one to three year," he said. "I last a while yet. Just hard sometimes. Episodes."

"Who else knows?"

"Jules, Tex, Ted, Sparky, Sam, and Ivan."

"And they let you sign up for this?"

"I force issue," he said, looking at her. "Dead soon anyway, why not fight for good? Fight for bad too many time in past. Maybe this erase some."

Kaylee's tears were running down her cheeks, and she shook as the sorrow took her. "Oh, Uncle." They hugged, both crying.

"I sorry," he said. "There more. Hang over me like death."

"What? Is auntie okay?"

"Your mom and dad," he said softly.

"Oh, God," she said, turning away from him, sobbing uncontrollably. He let her go for a few minutes.

"What happened?" she asked, still turned away. He touched her shoulder and she shrugged it off.

"Enemy find," he said. "My brother sent message before they took them. Asked me to protect you. Told me not to tell until things better. That why I gather you and friends at house."

"Was he in on the war?" she asked.

"He was following North Korean nukes to terrorists," Ji-Ho said. "Told government. Government had him killed, then go after me."

She turned towards him, still crying. "You've been holding all of this to yourself. You should've told me before now. That's too hard."

"*This* hard," Ji-Ho said.

"Trevor. I knew you thought he'd be good for me. You must've been desperate."

"I was," Ji-Ho said. "Lucky to find him. Please don't hold against him."

"I already knew you were matchmaking," she said, looking at him with red eyes. "I told you to back off, remember?"

"You bonded now?" Ji-Ho asked.

A smile rose through her tears. "I'll be with him for the rest of my life. We're on the same page about that."

Ji-Ho smiled, shaking his head yes.

"What can I do to help you?"

"Have patience," Ji-Ho said. "I already better now. Be fine for days, then this again. Maybe should have somebody with me when driving battle wagon. Clem and Sarah. I talk to them."

"Yes, you do that. Do you want something to eat? I'll fix you something."

"No, you not nurse, I do fine. Please?"

"Okay, Uncle, but if there's ever any help that you need, please ask."

There was a knock at the door. "Ji-Ho, you know where Kaylee is?"

She got up and went to the door, opening it for him, pulling him into her arms.

"You've been crying," he said, looking into her red swollen eyes.

"I've got a lot to tell you about," she whispered.

"Hi, Trevor," Ji-Ho said, walking slowly out of the bedroom.

"You don't look so good," Trevor said.

"I'm getting better. Kaylee tell you what going on. We have meeting, I bet."

"Half an hour," Trevor said.

"Good, then let me get ready. I see you in while."

Kaylee looked at Trevor, and nodded at the door. They went back to their coach.

***

Saladin sat in the cave, going over battle plans with his top lieutenants. The location was getting to him. Capitol Reef had its charms, but it was dusty and hot, with all manner of disgusting insects and rodents making themselves known at the worst of times. His phone rang. He looked at the screen. "I must take this. Leadership. Carry on." He walked out with it to his ear, into the mid-day Utah heat.

"Liking the desert?" Daan asked.

"What do you want?"

"Sorry, couldn't resist. I'm not liking where I am all that much either, by the way."

"And that is?"

"The great southwest," Daan said.

"That doesn't narrow things down much. I'm in the great southwest myself. Not sure what's so *great* about it."

Daan chuckled. "The rest of your men make it to Utah okay?"

"They're all here. We're planning a surprise attack on the Kansas base, which my sources tell me isn't much of a base at all."

"Never underestimate this enemy," Daan said.

"What's on your mind? I'm busy."

"The UN and the EU got their differences ironed out," Daan said. "They're sending more troops to California, and that's not all."

"The US Navy is still out there," Saladin said. "And don't forget those pesky citizens."

"Ivan's moved everything he has into the south. He thinks that's his main problem. We took out his social media team last night."

"Ben Dover's team? Is he dead?"

"We don't know for sure yet," Daan said. "Probably. When our commandos attacked and tried to take possession of their computer equipment, it all blew up. We don't control the Sacramento authorities right now, so we're waiting for official information on the bodies. I've heard it's hard to tell the remains of one person from another. Probably a DNA job."

"He's still alive. He detonated the bomb."

"We're thinking more like booby trap, but we'll see. It doesn't matter."

"It does matter, because Ben Dover will start a new team quickly," Saladin said. "I've seen reports on the movement of citizens down to the border. They've got an impressive number there already."

"And you know the troops headed north aren't your best," Daan said. "Even with significantly larger numbers, they'll have a hard time winning."

"That's why I wanted to take the two hundred thousand down there."

"You stay on General Hogan," Daan said. "We've got another plan in the works right now."

"Are you going to tell me what it is? I'm not seeing the point of this conversation."

"We're moving the good troops up into central Mexico to crush the US Army and their Mexican allies," Daan said.

"On whose authority? We need those troops to finish our conquest of Argentina, Brazil, Columbia, and all of those stupid Central American countries that I can't remember the names of."

"They'll be back down there soon enough, and we aren't moving all of them. Just the best ones."

"You've been watching the reports from down there, right?" Saladin asked. "The locals are starting to organize better. They've been watching Ivan the Butcher and some of the other nationalist scum who are still active."

"Minor problem," Daan said.

"It wasn't so minor up here."

"Yes, but down there the citizenry isn't armed, and they're used to taking orders from whoever is in charge. Add to that the fact that there's nobody running guns to them, and that makes the resistance insignificant."

"Remember the Viet Cong?" Saladin asked. "You damn Europeans learn nothing from history."

"Says the man who thinks we'll all eventually bend the knee to Allah," Daan cracked. "Whatever. We need you to work strategy with the forces down there. They need some perspective, and when you aren't doing something stupid, you have a good handle on things."

"I'm going to hang up now."

"No, you're not," Daan said. "Right now your reputation is crap, but it won't be if you cooperate with us on this. I'm giving you a life line. I wish I could move you there. Your chances of survival would be better."

"Why?"

"George Franklin and General Hogan," Daan said. "Forget about them already?"

Saladin was silent for a moment.

"I can tell that you haven't," Daan said. "Healthy."

"I'm angry, not scared," he spat.

"Then you aren't as smart as I thought you were."

"Have you forgotten about the US Army in Mexico?" Saladin asked.

"Have you forgotten that the leadership running the Mexican campaign is part of the coalition, which is on our side? We'll turn on the nationalists in the Mexican government. We'll root them all out and take over. Then we can renew attacks on the US mainland from over the border, as we were doing so successfully before."

"That coalition is falling apart, and the US Government, regardless of what they say, aren't helping," Saladin said. "They're dragging their feet every step of the way."

"The US Government feels the urgency of moving more quickly," Daan said. "We put the fear of God into them."

"You're thinking that the attack on southern California is a diversion," Saladin said. "That's too many men to waste on such a risky venture, even if they aren't our best men."

"It's only partly a diversion. We'll still overrun the border and re-take major parts of eastern San Diego County. Then we'll stage for an assault on western San Diego County, but we'll have to time it with the arrival of more troops. We'll probably lose a lot of that force, but no matter. A victory here and there will lull our enemy."

"You guys are delusional," Saladin said. One of his people scurried over to him with a note. He looked at it and laughed. "If I were you I'd abandon this stupid plan and pull the South American troops back where they can hold some ground."

"Why?"

"The US Marines are shelling our troops. You guys put them someplace where they have no cover. It's gonna be a bloodbath before they even get close to the damn border."

Daan was silent for a moment.

"You there?" Saladin asked.

"I need to make a few calls."

{14}

The Livery Stable

Jules woke up from a long sleep, the feeling of panic hitting him as he reached for Shelley on her empty side of the bed. He picked up his phone. It was already 10:00. The sound of women laughing approached, and then he could hear Shelley, Dana, and Karen chatting happily. The door of the coach opened, Shelley walking to the bedroom.

"Meeting coming up, honey. Time to get up."

"Yes, I know," he said, getting out of bed and stretching. "Walking the grounds?"

"This place is a full-on riot. It's like a movie set, except it's all real."

"I like. The saloon was fun."

She watched as he got dressed. "Want a cup of coffee to take along?"

"Sure, in paper cup if we still have," he said, sitting on the bed to tie his shoes.

"We still do." She turned on the generator, then went into the kitchen as he finished.

"Who's running meeting?" Jules asked, taking the warm paper cup from Shelley's hands.

"Our host and somebody named Sam. They're holding it in a barn at the end of main street."

"Good," Jules said, sipping the coffee. "Get enough sleep?"

"I did. You?"

"Yes. Glad I didn't hang around the saloon too late last night."

They headed for the door, Jules shutting down the generator before they left.

"We gonna get hookups?" Shelly asked.

"Not ask yet," Jules said. "We talk about later. Might not happen until after battle. Coach fuel tank full, so generator is good fall back."

They left the large pasture, rows of battle wagons on either side. Their friends were coming out, all heading for the main street, a block away to the north.

"I love this place," Tex said, walking next to them with Karen, Sparky, and Dana.

Karen snickered. "He's home."

"Well, it's not Texas, but it does have a certain charm," he said.

"Most of the off-roaders got here early this morning," Sparky said. "Woke me up. I need a little more sleep."

"Anxious to see upgrades," Jules said. "Did you look?"

"Not yet. What were they gonna do to them?" Sparky asked.

"Armor around driver and passenger, and new main gun."

"New main gun?" Tex asked. "Those grenade launchers aren't enough?"

"Ever hear of XM214 microgun?" Jules asked.

"I remember those," Sparky said.

"My mind's drawing a blank on that one, partner," Tex said.

"They cancelled that program," Sparky said.

"Is somebody gonna tell me what it is?" Tex asked. Karen laughed, rolling her eyes.

Jules chuckled. "Mini gun that fire .223 ammo."

"Holy crap," Tex said. "Seriously?"

"Yes, plans from GE's original program. Ivan set up shop. Use 3-D printers for parts and mount. Attach to existing M19 grenade launcher."

"I'm interested," Tex said. "Suppose we get hand-held versions of those? Probably kick less than an M60 or a BAR. The rate of fire would make up for the lower-power round."

"I request," Jules said. "Ivan say no. Unit weigh 35 pounds. Also need power source. Too much to carry, no?"

Sparky laughed. "I'm not up to that. I'll stick with my trusty M60. That's heavy enough."

They rounded the corner, getting onto the wooden sidewalk of the main street.

"I smell food," Shelley said.

"Have more appetite now, huh?" Karen asked. Shelley shot her a sharp glare. Nobody else seemed to notice.

"I see barn," Jules said. "Sign say *Livery Stable*. Where O.K. Corral?"

Tex chuckled. "Look, horses." He nodded to several which were tied up in front of the saloon.

"Where are Ji-Ho's battle wagons?" Sparky asked.

"We saw some on the far end of town," Shelley said, "where we walked this morning. They've got hookups over there, but it doesn't look like there's room for more coaches."

"How many were there?" Tex asked.

"About twenty," Karen said. "Some of them looked brand new."

"Yes, Ivan send more," Jules said.

"Listen," Sparky said, slowing. "That sounds like a chopper."

"Oh, crap, maybe we should have our guns with us," Karen said.

"Probably Ivan," Jules said. He whipped out his phone and sent a text. It dinged with a reply in seconds. "Yes, Ivan and Ben. Came from local airport."

They watched as the chopper came down in the field behind the streets.

"You want to go meet them, honey?" Shelley asked.

"No, we see in barn."

They walked past the rest of the street, getting onto a dirt path between the end of the wooden sidewalk and the barn. Sam was outside with Garrett, Clem, and Sid, welcoming the crowd as they came in.

"Good morning," Jules said.

Sam smiled. "Great to see you guys. There's food on the long tables just inside the door."

"Thanks, partner," Tex said.

They entered, got some food, and carried their paper plates to benches set up in front, the first row already occupied. Robbie and Morgan were there, sitting next to Justin and Katie.

Karen sat next to Shelley and made eye contact, then moved close to whisper. "Sorry."

Shelley shrugged, whispering back. "Nobody noticed."

Seth and Kaitlyn came in and sat behind them, Angel and Megan joining. Trevor and Kaylee showed up a moment later, Megan freezing when she saw Kaylee's puffy eyes.

"What's wrong?" she asked.

"I'll tell you after this," Kaylee said. Trevor glanced at Megan, hurt in his eyes, then put his arm around Kaylee's shoulders and pulled her close.

Ed came in with Ryan and Tyler. Erica followed, but moved towards the front to be next to Sam instead of sitting with them. Anna showed up a moment later, going to Garrett.

The barn filled quickly, and then there was commotion at the door. Jules turned, his face breaking into a broad smile as he saw Ivan and Ben walking up the center isle with Garrett, Sam, and Ji-Ho. Ivan had on his usual pin-striped suit with fedora, looking well pressed.

The crowd hushed as Garrett got on the small platform, taking the podium. He tapped the microphone, which sounded throughout the large space. "Sounds like it's on. Welcome, everybody. Glad you could make it. There's plenty of food, so don't be shy."

"Thanks!" said somebody from the back. Others muttered in agreement. The crowd got silent again.

"I'd like to introduce two of our friends. I know all of you have heard of them, maybe seen them on video too, but this is the first time most of you have seen them in person. Ivan and Ben. Come on up here, guys!"

Ivan came up, tipping his hat to the audience as the crowd roared, Ben following him, looking embarrassed at the attention.

"You all should be proud of yourselves," Ivan began. "You've been the driving force in the victories we've had over the Islamists and the UN. Thanks to you, our state is well on the way to stamping out their operations completely. Together we'll work to finish the job as quickly as possible, so we can all go back to our normal lives."

The people cheered, Ivan waiting, looking at the crowd, then over at Garrett and the others. He spoke again when they were quiet.

"We have a great battle starting as we speak, to the south. We are facing some terrible odds, but we have more help than we had in the past. The US Navy and the Marines are joining us this time. Most of you know that there are three-quarters of a million enemy troops walking towards the border. Marine artillery is pounding them right now. They won't have those numbers for long. That doesn't mean the battle is won, though. Not by a long shot. Many of these invaders will get through, and many people on both sides will be killed or wounded."

He looked out over the quiet crowd for a moment.

"I believe we will win this battle, and win it big. The enemy will not get their new supply of troops to rescue those trapped here after their numerous defeats. We will halt the advance of the invaders, and then root out the remaining enemy fighters from all over the state."

"Are we going down there to join the battle?" asked Cody, from the middle of the crowd.

"That remains to be seen," Ivan said. "We're well dug in along the border, and very well armed. Along with the artillery we're using there, the area between Old Highway 80 and the border is rigged with claymore mines, and we have hundreds of mortars set up. Trains have brought boxcar after boxcar of Marines into the area, as the multitude of citizens continue to arrive. Our biggest problem right now is that the major roads into the area are clogged with incoming recruits."

"What are we gonna do?" Angel asked. "If the roads are clogged, we won't be able to get our battle wagons down there."

"We'll be doing cleanup of any enemy fighters who get through, and we'll be a staging ground for the citizen recruits who are continuing to arrive. We'll also be handling re-supply of ammo and weapons as long as the battle rages."

"What's the Navy going to do to help?" asked Tyler.

"Two main things," Ivan said. "First, they'll insure that no EU ships land additional troops in this area. We know for a fact that the EU Navy is sending ships full of UN Peacekeepers, to re-take the parts of California they've lost. We'll destroy them before they get close."

"Who's minding the store up north now that you've moved down here?" Ed asked.

"I didn't bring my entire team down here," Ivan said, "and we've still got the citizenry who did most of the heavy lifting. We'll coordinate with them whenever we get news of a possible attack."

"What's the other thing the Navy is doing?" Trevor asked.

"Air support," Ivan said. "Their jets and helicopters will pound the enemy once they've gotten across the border, assuming some of them will."

The room broke into murmurs.

"Won't they hit some of our people if they wait until the enemy crosses the border?" Susanne asked, standing next to Elmer and Willard in the back.

"Special care will be taken to prevent losses due to friendly fire," Ivan said.

"They should've hit them south of the border," Willard said.

"I agree with that," Ivan said, "the Navy leadership is trying to prevent outside forces from joining the fight on the enemy side. They'd been warned against taking unilateral action outside of the United States."

"Yeah, but we're shelling the enemy while they're in Mexico," Seth said.

"True, and I must admit I was surprised about that," Ivan said. "Might just come down to explicit warnings."

Ed laughed. "This limited warfare crap is maddening. Reminds me of Nam. Is there anything we can do to change their minds?"

"I tried early on," Ivan said. "Since I've heard that some of the brass is upset with the shelling, I decided to avoid further comment for now. The shelling might be more effective anyway."

"We know there's still around three-hundred thousand Islamist spread out over the state," Seth said. "Our history program is showing their movements fairly well now. We can't see the UN Peacekeepers. Is there a similar number?"

"Ah, you must be Seth," Ivan said. "Heard good things about you and your partner Kaitlyn. Let's talk after this meeting. I'd like to get you, Robbie, and Ben together. There can be some synergy there, I think."

Seth smiled. "I'd love it. We've heard great things about both."

"Good," Ivan said. "Now, to your question. The UN's forces have been hit hard, but as you know, they have not been destroyed. I heard about the attack just yesterday on this facility. The good news is that we have them on the run, and we estimate there are less than fifty thousand UN Peacekeepers left on California soil."

"The way you said that, I'm expecting some bad news to counter it," Ed said.

"The EU and the UN were having a spat over funding and personnel losses," Ivan said. "That's the main reason they were unable to re-supply their forces in the last couple weeks. They've set their differences aside for now. As I mentioned, there are troop transport ships cruising to the USA as we speak."

"Just California?" Trevor asked.

"Our sources tell us they're also attempting to bring forces and supplies to the Eastern seaboard, to shore up martial law in the Mid-Atlantic and New England."

"Our Navy will be spread thin," Ed said.

"They will, but our Navy is many times larger than the EU Navy, and what's left of the Royal Navy has joined us. We stand a good chance of being victorious. I won't candy-coat this and say there's no danger, though. We're still in this war, and there are a lot of moving parts. The US Navy is one big one."

"What about the US Airforce?" Cody asked. "And the US Army?"

"The US Army is tied up in Mexico, for the most part, but we expect that situation to come to an end soon. The US Airforce is beginning to get involved now, thanks to certain treasonous Pentagon leaders leaving the country over the last several days."

"So, it sounds like our main job in the immediate future is helping with staging and supply, and being ready to back up the forces to the south," Tyler said.

"Yes," Ivan said.

Garrett stood up. "We've got another concern, as most of you know."

"Please, come take the mic," Ivan said. "I've said what I wanted to say. I'll be here if there are more questions."

Garrett nodded and walked to the front. "Even though the UN Peacekeeper force has been weakened, they're still around, and still causing us problems. Add to that the fact that they've tried to bring Islamists in lead-shielded vehicles once already, and that makes us somewhat vulnerable."

Murmurs rose from the crowd.

"On the good side, we have a lot more fighters now, and we have a lot more firepower too," Garrett said. "It would take an extremely large force to overrun us in a battle. A small number of enemy fighters could sneak in with mortars again and shell the town. We need to focus on that. I'm getting together with Sid after we're done here, to use his excellent tracking ability yet again. We need to find out how the UN Peacekeepers got in here. Anybody who'd like to help would be welcome."

Sam stood up and walked to the podium. "We have many upgraded off-roaders. I think we should add them to the patrols until we lock this down."

"What kind of upgrades did they get?" Trevor asked.

Ji-Ho smiled and came up, joining the others around the mic. "XM214 microguns, mounted on top of existing M19s."

Trevor laughed. "Those never made it to production. How'd we manage that?"

Ivan smiled and turned back to the mic. "We got GE's original plans and used our 3D printing capability to create them, with a little help from our machine shop."

"What's an XM214?" Robbie asked.

"It's a small mini gun which fires .223 ammo," Sam said. "Nice little unit."

"They work well," shouted one of the off-roaders from the back. "I'd say they expanded our capability by more than a hundred percent."

"Let's get some of your team set up to start patrols, then, provided Garrett has no objection."

Garrett smiled, walking back to the mic. "I think it's a great idea, but we will keep the mounted patrols running as well, in areas where it's difficult for off-roaders to operate."

"Sounds great," Ivan said. "Does anybody have any questions?"

Seth stood up. "We heard a rumor that Ben lost his team last night. Is that true?"

Ben nodded, walking up to the mic. "I'm afraid so. We had a plant in our ranks, and he led a UN commando team right to us, as we were getting ready to leave our Sacramento location."

"You lost friends," Seth said. "I'm sorry."

"It's hard, but we're in a war," Ben said. "We've got replacement equipment. How'd you like to help us set it up?"

"Love too," Seth said. "Kaitlyn can help too. She's good with that stuff as well."

Jules made eye contact with Robbie, who stood up. "I'll help out too, if you'd like. This is right up my alley."

"Then let's do it," Ben said.

"I've got a good place, if this operation needs to be protected," Elmer said.

"You aren't thinking of giving them the reloading facility, are ya?" Susanne asked.

"Yes, as a matter of fact," Elmer said.

"Susanne, we're flush with guns and ammo now," Willard said, "and we've still got massive reserves of black powder ammo in the storage room. There's more important things you can do."

"You guys are taking my job away," Susanne said.

"We've got better job for you," Ji-Ho said. "Load .223 rounds onto belts. Labor intensive. Perfect."

"There's a great idea," Garrett said. "Just as important, and a far cry safer too. You won't run the risk of blowing yourself up doing that."

Several people in the audience cracked up.

"Oh, all right," she said. "I think we ought to get all of the percussion caps and primers out of the mine, then. No use risking an explosion."

"I'll help you, honey," Elmer said.

"Actually, we'll need you to work on the electrical for the PCs, and some lighting," Garrett said.

Suzanne nodded. "Okay, I'll have my ladies help me cart the primers away. There's another room down there we can use to do the belt stuffing. We'll need lights down there too."

"You could do it on the surface," Elmer said.

Susanne shook her head no. "Cooler in the mine."

"Wait, you're talking about us setting up underground?" Ben asked.

"Yep," Willard said. "You ain't claustrophobic, are ya?"

Ben laughed. "No, it'll be fine, as long as it's not too damp for the equipment down there."

"It's not," Susanne said. "Couldn't have used it for black powder reloading if it was. That stuff soaks up moisture like a sponge."

"Okay, then I say we break into teams and get to work," Garrett said.

"Let's meet someplace for a while, gentlemen," Ivan said, looking at Sam, Ji-Ho, Garrett, and the others in the leadership team.

"We can use the saloon," Willard said. "I'll open her up."

"Perfect," Sam said, looking at Ivan. "You're gonna love this place."

"I'm sure," Ivan said.

The group finished up and left the barn.

{15}

Underground

The artillery barrage continued, guns firing into the Mexican desert, the gunners watching the apps and adjusting on the fly.

Conrad walked over to Lieutenant Colonel Meyers. "You see what the enemy is doing?"

"Yeah," Meyers said. "They're fanning out wide."

"Won't that mean we lose our funnel? Our kill zone with the Claymore mines?"

Meyers shook his head no. "They'll try to re-funnel once they get too close for our artillery to be effective. This is the point closest to the road. They'll try to steal vehicles if we're defeated. Wish they were further away."

"You're saying we shouldn't fan our men out wider?" Conrad asked.

Meyers thought silently for a moment. "Let's look at the map. You have a good handle on where the citizens are?"

"Fairly good."

Meyers walked to his tent with Conrad, reaching in to get his tablet. He pulled up the map program and they looked at it.

"What are you guys up to?" Doug asked, walking over with Jorge.

"Trying to figure out strategy now that the enemy is fanning out so wide," Conrad said.

"You know where the backup in traffic is, right?" Meyers asked.

Doug shook his head yes. "Some of our people took their motorcycles up to the blockage points. It's still Ocotillo to the east and Boulder Oaks to the west."

They all gathered close, looking at the table, trying to block the glare of the sun.

"The enemy must have some intelligence on Highway 94," Jorge said. "Look how many are going to that side."

"Let me see that," Meyers asked, taking Jorge's phone. "Dammit, that isn't good."

"How close are we to having that route open?" Conrad asked.

"We have one of the motorcycle teams heading in that direction," Doug said. "I'll text them. Might be a while. Takes two hands to ride."

"Please do," Meyers said. "I better make some calls."

"Wait, let's chat a minute longer," Conrad said.

"What's on your mind?" Meyers asked.

"We don't have enough room for everybody who's coming, even if we didn't have the traffic tie-up," he said. "I say we get people coming down Buckman Springs Road and the other smaller roads going south from I-8. Get them to the border. If they need to come east to help us right here, they can do that easy enough, but if the enemy is going to try for Highway 94, they'll be there to stop it."

"Will they have the numbers and firepower to make any difference?" Jorge asked.

Conrad smiled. "Ivan's forces arrived at Dodge City last night, along with all of those crazy battle wagons and off-roaders. I say we ask them to get on Highway 94 as soon as they can get through the pass."

"We should do the same thing on the east side," Jorge said. "Let's start running them south from Ocotillo on the small roads through the Jacumba Wilderness. They won't make it here in time anyway, and once they're to the border, they can use the road along the fence to come in this direction if we need them."

"I like it," Meyers said. "It will keep the enemy from being able to encircle our position here."

"We're liable to lose a lot of civilians doing this," Doug said.

"We're gonna lose a lot of civilians no matter what we do," Conrad said. "Knew the gig when we took it."

"Some of the enemy fighters are gonna get through," Jorge said.

"Yep, right into the multitude of citizens who are still on the way," Conrad said.

"And they'll have to contend with our air power then," Meyers said. "Okay, I'm gonna make some calls. Conrad, you got some inroads with Ivan's folks?"

"Yes sir," Conrad said. "I'll get them on the horn."

Doug pulled his phone out, looking at it with a wide grin. "That pass on Highway 94 is open."

***

Elmer led Robbie, Seth, Kaitlyn, and Ben into the mine, all of them with heavy backpacks on. It got cooler as they got deeper, the dim LED lights along the ceiling putting off an eerie glow.

"Find many artifacts down here?" Robbie asked, "other than the whiskey, that is?"

Elmer chuckled. "There's stuff all over the place, but we've just left it."

"You guys found whiskey down here?" Ben asked.

"Lots," Elmer said. "We haven't even brought all of it out yet."

"It's good stuff," Seth said. "Real good." Kaitlyn nodded in agreement.

"Those buildings aren't old, are they?" Ben asked.

Elmer turned to him, slowing down. "When we bought this land, all that was here were ruins along main street, and the mine, which had been closed up with dynamite somewhere along the line."

"So, you built the western town right on top of the ruins?" Ben asked.

"Pretty much," Elmer said. "Here's the place I had in mind." They entered a room, carved out with a higher ceiling than the tunnel they'd come out of. There were metal folding tables along the wall, more in the center. Reloading presses and boxes of lead bullets sat near the door. "Looks like Susanne still has some stuff to move, but it won't get in our way."

"Did you make the town look like the original?" Seth asked.

"I was wondering that too," Kaitlyn said.

"We found a few old pictures, and used them as a guide," Elmer said. "Parts of the original rebuild got torn down, though. Garrett and the others didn't know anything about permits.'

Ben cracked up. "Dangerous thing in nanny-state California."

"You got that right," Elmer said. "That's how I hooked up with these folks originally. Knew a few of them. I'm a contractor. I helped them fix what was fixable and build new structures where the original wasn't salvageable."

"Why did they build the town?" Ben asked.

"Originally? Reenactments, mainly. These folks are kinda like Civil War reenactors. That's why they got so deep into the black powder guns and such."

"Did they plan to live here originally?" Kaitlyn asked. "I remember reading about this place. There didn't used to be many full-time residents."

"No, that happened when things started to go sideways. Garrett lived here before we bought the rest of the land, on his ranch outside of town. That's been in the family for over a hundred years. When the rest of the land came on the market, he got together his group and made a pitch to pool resources and buy it, but it was mainly for recreation. The land was cheap."

"Who owned it?" Robbie asked.

"Mining company," Elmer said, "actually, a holding company that received the land after the mining company went out of business. The family that owned the original company died off. Mines around here been played out for years, of course. There was some question if anybody from the twentieth century even knew the company held this land."

"Interesting," Robbie said. "Good fodder for a novel."

"You're a writer, huh?" Ben asked.

"Yeah, but haven't had much time for it lately."

Ben laughed. "I'm a political writer. Haven't been able to pursue that lately either."

"We'll get back to it," Robbie said.

"What do you think, guys?" Elmer asked. "Can you work down here?"

"What about cellphone reception?" Ben asked.

"We put a repeater out there, so we could communicate with Susanne when she was running her operation down here. We might want to expand it a little bit. Got internet lines running down here already, too."

"Why'd you do that?" Kaitlyn asked.

"Early on, we thought it better to have a place to hole up. Didn't think we'd have the resources to fight back. Californians stepped up."

"You haven't been eight hundred people for long, then?" Seth asked.

"Nah. The core group was about a hundred and twenty. Hell, I wasn't even a part of the original group."

"Who was?" Kaitlyn asked.

"Garrett and his family, which includes Susanne, of course. Willard, and a bunch of reenacting weekend warriors, mainly. We have a group of theater folks here–that's how we were able to do the shows."

"Shows?" Ben asked.

"They had an old-west opera house going," Kaitlyn said. "We sent business their way from our casino. I went once. It was fun."

"Those people still here?" Robbie asked.

"Most of them, but we don't encourage strangers to come here right now," Elmer said. "No more shows for a while. I hope we get back to it. Susanne was big-time into that. I think she's cranky because she can't do it now."

"You'll get back to it someday," Kaitlyn said, "and we'll get our casino business back too."

Elmer smiled. "Hope so."

There were footsteps approaching. Clem and Sarah appeared at the door way, Morgan with them, a backpack slung over one shoulder. She rushed over to Robbie's side.

"Figured you guys might want some wiring done," Clem said. "Need any help, Elmer?"

"Hell yeah," Elmer said. "You know more about that than me, I suspect."

"Who wired this place with the cell repeater and Wi-Fi originally?" Seth asked.

"Contractors from town," Elmer said. "Murdered by the enemy during their first wave through here."

"Bastards," Clem said. "I'm ready to dig in any time."

Sarah smiled. "Yeah, I'd rather have you doing this than stomping around in the back country with Sid and the others."

Clem chuckled. "I knew why you suggested it, but I'm glad you did. I'm more good here anyway."

"Oh, didn't want him exposed to more snipers, eh?" Morgan asked. "Good."

"I saw you," Ben said, looking at Morgan in the dim light. "On the TV, when you and the others testified about the UN captivity. Your courage impressed the hell out of me."

Morgan shot him an embarrassed look.

"Sorry, didn't mean to make you uncomfortable."

"It's okay, Ben," she said. "I'm glad I did it. Most of the others are here too."

"Then we're in good company," Ben said.

"I saw the video of you too, Ben," Robbie said. "The right thing at the right time. Very brave. I'm in awe."

"Likewise," Seth said.

"Well, I'd be dead if not for Ivan," Ben said, "more than once."

Seth took off his backpack, and started pulling computer equipment out, setting it on a table. "This okay?"

"Go for it," Elmer said. "There's enough power strips to get started."

"You want to use Wi-Fi down here, or ethernet lines?" Clem asked, looking at the wiring coming in.

"Either would work for us," Kaitlyn said.

"Whatever is faster," Ben said. "We're gonna have a lot of conversations going on. We'll need to expand this team, too. You guys know that, right?"

"How many people are you thinking?" Elmer asked. "Matters for the electrical."

"I'd like at least eight more," Ben said.

"Okay, I'll wire it for that," Elmer said.

Susanne came in with a few ladies, picking up the remainder of the supplies. "How's it going?"

"I think this will work," Elmer said. "Sorry to displace you."

"Ah, hell, you were right, you old bushwhacker," she said. "We're setting up shop in the mill instead of down here. Those ammo belts are too heavy to carry around, and we don't have the explosion issues anymore."

"I thought you wanted to be cool," Elmer said.

"The mill has those swamp coolers, remember?"

"Oh, yeah," Elmer said. "That'll help. I'll be up there after this to make sure you got everything you need."

"Thanks," she said. "C'mon, girls, let's go." She paused, seeing Sarah standing next to Clem, and came over.

"Hi, Susanne," Sarah said, looking nervous.

"I saw you moved," she said softly. "Sorry about last night."

"No worries. I actually like being closer to Clem, but don't spread that around too much."

"I had a feeling," she said, a sly grin on her face. "Enjoy. No hard feelings."

Sarah nodded, and Susanne turned and joined her group, picking up a box of shell casings.

"Glad that's over with," Sarah whispered. Clem nodded, touching her shoulder.

"Me too. Want to help me with this?"

"What can I do?" Sarah asked.

"Probably help me to pull wires. We might need to go into town."

She giggled. "Oh, we're going to Scooter's again?"

Elmer laughed. "Oh, you met old Scooter, huh? He's well stocked, but he talks your ear off. You ask him what time it is and he tells you how to build a watch."

Clem laughed. "Yeah, I noticed. I need to pace this out to see how much cable I'll need. Want to show me where the internet source is?"

"Sure," Elmer said. "Let's go." The three left the room.

"Can you tell me about this history program of yours?" Ben asked, walking over to Seth.

"Yeah, I'm interested in that too." Robbie said.

They pulled up chairs next to Seth's table.

"I'll show you," Seth said. He opened the program.

"Better run it, honey," Kaitlyn said. "We didn't run an AM report today, with all the excitement."

Seth nodded, clicking on the report button. "This will take a little while. We've got a pretty good dataset. Wish we had a strong desktop system to run this on."

"That's a gamer laptop, at least," Robbie said, looking at it.

"It is, but it just doesn't have the raw power."

"What is your program doing?" Ben asked.

"It takes a snapshot of all the enemy hits within the region every few minutes. We're using outside servers to crunch and store the raw data."

"Outside servers?" Robbie asked. "That safe?"

"Yeah," Seth said. "It's all encrypted, which is part of the computing power issue."

"Why does it matter how powerful the local machine is, then?" Ben asked.

"Kaitlyn is an Excel expert," Seth said. "She developed a reporting tool, which takes about sixty pages of VB code to run. That takes a while with this machine."

"What's your program telling you that you can't see by running the apps live?" Robbie asked.

"We originally developed this so we could watch for Islamists disappearing and reappearing," Kaitlyn said.

"Why?" Ben asked.

"We got attacked by Islamists in lead-shielded vans," Seth said. "It was two UN Peacekeepers driving, the back shielded part of the van full of Islamist fighters. Got the drop on us a couple times. We were afraid they'd expand that capability, and we wanted some warning. If a whole bunch of these cretins disappear all of a sudden, we know there's something up."

"I get it," Morgan said. "They can't just hide themselves. If they leave an area, you'll see them. If they drop off the screen completely, you'll know they've effectively hidden themselves."

"Yep, and we'll know what the numbers are, too," Kaitlyn said.

"Genius, man," Ben said.

"How big of an area do you cover?" Robbie asked.

"We've got it set to a thousand square miles," Seth said. "That's why it's taking so long to run."

"Wow," Ben said, squinting at the screen as the computer chugged away at the data.

"Maybe we should talk about our strengths, so we can decide who does what," Robbie said.

Ben smiled. "Good idea."

"Agreed," Kaitlyn said, looking at Seth, who shook his head yes, eyes glued to the laptop screen.

"I'm good at copy writing," Robbie said. "I'd rather write fiction, but I made money on the side writing text that would draw people in, and it worked."

"So, when we start recruitment, you'd be key to draw interest," Ben said. "We had a person like that in the last team, and she was essential."

"Did you lose her in the ambush?" Robbie asked.

Ben nodded yes, trying to keep the emotion from taking him.

"Seth and I are good with technical stuff," Kaitlyn said. "Data gathering and analysis."

"That's obvious," Ben said. "I know the internet community like the back of my hand. I know where to kick things off, who to enlist to help us get the word out, and so on. Got that ability as a campus radical."

"You were a campus radical?" Robbie asked. "You mean like SDS?"

Ben laughed. "No, more like the *Sons of Liberty*."

The laptop beeped.

"It's done, honey," Kaitlyn said, turning to see him staring at the screen, already opening the report.

"Dammit," he said. "We've got to talk to Garrett and the others."

"You see something?" Robbie asked.

"Julian. About seven hundred enemy fighters vanished overnight. Wish I would've run this before we went into the meeting."

"They can't hide that many people in shielded vehicles, can they?" Morgan asked.

Seth looked at her, brow furrowed. He went to his browser, typing in the search window. Robbie pulled his phone out and sent a text.

"Who are you texting to?" Ben asked.

"Jules," Robbie said. "He'll spread the word around."

"Crap," Seth said.

"What?" Kaitlyn asked, getting closer to him, looking at the laptop screen.

"What's it say?" Ben asked.

"I searched on how many people fit in a semi-trailer."

"Oh," Ben said. "And?"

"In a two-trailer rig, the number is over five hundred," he said, looking back at them. "This page is about illegal immigrant smugglers."

"Son of a bitch," Robbie said. "They could get seven hundred folks here in two semi rigs."

"How far is Julian from here?" Morgan asked.

Robbie pulled out his phone and loaded the GPS program. "Worst case, a couple hours. They're probably already here."

"No," Kaitlyn said.

Robbie's phone dinged with a text.

"Jules?" Morgan asked.

"Yeah, he's mobilizing everybody," Robbie said.

"Should we get out there?" Ben asked.

"No, they want us to keep watching this," Robbie said. He kicked off the report again, adjusting the range down to two-hundred square miles. "It'll run a lot faster at this setting."

"I'll get set up," Ben said, pulling the laptop out of his backpack.

"I'm doing the same," Robbie said.

Morgan glanced at Kaitlyn. "Let's go grab our guns, just in case."

"You run your report," Seth said, getting out of the chair. "I'll go do that–I'll grab your AK and my M60."

"I'll help," Morgan said, looking at Robbie, who nodded yes.

{16}

Gravel

Sid, Sam, Ed, Tyler, Ryan, and Garrett were moving slowly through the back of the Dodge City property in the Jeep Unlimited with its top down, eyes peeled at the tracks coming from behind the ridge.

"Here it is," Sid said. "Stop. I'm getting out."

Sam nodded, parking the vehicle. Everybody got out, M60s or M4s in hand.

"There's an old stagecoach route back here," Garrett said. "This trail runs into it after a couple miles."

"Is it drivable?" Ed asked.

Garrett thought for a moment. "It's rutted as hell in spots, but any four-wheel-drive vehicle could handle it. A heavy-duty two-wheel drive could handle most of it."

"Where does it go?" Tyler asked.

"Off our land," Garrett said. "Across Mother Grundy Truck Trail Road, and on into Deerhorn Valley. It kinda links up with Honey Springs Road."

"Kinda?" Sid asked, stopping.

"There's a gap between this road and the highway, because of a seasonal creek. Used to go through originally, but I read that every year it got washed out. They eventually moved the stagecoach route someplace else. I'd be surprised if that little van could hack it."

"We should follow this all the way," Sid said. "Are there any forks before the stagecoach road?"

"Nothing but hiking trails," Garrett said.

"Good, then let's go," Sid said.

Sam got behind the wheel again, Sid riding shotgun, the rest getting in back. They drove forward.

"How far to your property line?" Ed asked, looking at Garrett.

"Couple miles, give or take."

"Hell of a spread," Tyler said. "This is almost as big as our reservation."

"Heard anything about your reservation?" Garrett asked. "I sure would like to go to your casino again."

Ed's expression was sad. "I hope we have enough left of the tribe to re-open it after this."

"We will," Ryan said. "Trust me."

"I hope you're right," Ed said.

They road silently for a while, crossing over Mother Grundy Truck Trail Road, heading outside of Garrett's land. The sun was higher in the sky, the heat hitting them harder with the top off the Jeep.

"Should've brought a hat," Sam said.

"You need one of these," Garrett said, tipping his cowboy hat.

"Maybe so," Sam replied.

"Slow down," Sid said.

Sam took his foot off the accelerator. "You see something?"

Sid nodded. "What's with the grayish white pebbles all of a sudden?"

"What grayish white pebbles?" Garrett asked.

"Stop the Jeep," Sid said. Sam put on the brakes and Sid jumped out, walking to one of them. He picked it up and brought it over.

"Crap, that looks like it came from a gravel road," Garrett said, eyes darting around.

"Maybe somebody filled that creek you were talking about with gravel, so they could drive across it," Sid said.

"Son of a bitch," Garrett said. "They're building a road back here."

"Who owns this land?" Sam asked.

"It's BLM. Tried to petition to buy it, but the Feds wouldn't have it. They tried to force us off our land at one point, to get us to back off."

"Interesting," Sid said. "Wonder why?"

"I thought it was because of the stagecoach road, and the ruins on our land. Knowing what I know about those cretins now, could've been anything."

"Let's keep going," Sid said.

The men got back in the Jeep, seeing more of the gravel as they rolled forward, the terrain turning from flat into rolling hills, the road rising and falling ahead of them.

***

Ivan's meeting in the saloon was just ending, when his cellphone buzzed. He looked at it, then held up his hand. "Hold it a minute. This is from one of our contacts on the southern border. I'll put it on speaker."

Ivan answered and pushed the speaker button. "This is Ivan."

"Ivan, how are you? This is Conrad."

"I'm good. You're on speaker, and I've got team members in the room. How's things down by Jacumba?"

"It's turned into a big city," he said. "You heard we were using artillery on the enemy, right?"

"Yeah, we heard," Ivan said. "What's on your mind?"

"We heard that Highway 94 was open again, and wanted to suggest that you bring your battle wagons and off-roaders down that way. The enemy is fanning out wide due to the artillery. We see a pretty large group heading for the area south of Tierra Del Sol Road."

"I know where that is," Willard said.

"You sure we want to pull everything away from here, partner?" Tex asked. "We've got a lot of people and supplies to protect."

"I wouldn't bring them all," Conrad said. "What do you have?"

Jules came closer. "We have forty-five off-roaders, and thirty-three battle wagons. How many men head to that spot?"

"Hard to tell exactly," Conrad said. "Couple hundred thousand. It's the extreme western tip of the enemy advance. We're bringing people straight south from Ocotillo as well, to widen our presence on the border."

"No more than half, no?" Jules said.

Ivan glanced over at him, then looked at the phone. "We need to discuss this. How far is the enemy from the border right now?"

"Thirty miles, but they've slowed down, now that we've scattered them with the artillery."

Ted looked up from his phone. "Yeah, that's what I'm seeing on the apps.

"Me too," Sparky said. "The center section is a little ahead of the west and east tips."

"That's where we have our biggest concentration of men," Conrad said. "I'll let you go."

"Talk to you soon," Ivan said. He ended the call, then sat back down. "I guess we're not done after all."

"So it would appear," Sparky said.

"We can't make an agreement on this without Sam, Ed, Garrett, and Sid," Erica said.

"I agree," Jules said.

Tex nodded, taking off his hat and running a hand through his hair. "Yep."

Ivan was silent for a moment, thinking.

"You think it's okay to go ahead without them, partner?" Tex asked.

"No, no," Ivan said, "I agree with the concerns. The entire leadership team must agree on this. I'm leaning against it, truth be told."

"Why?"

"What we'll face down there is a multitude of enemy fighters on foot, spread out in a wide area. They'll dig in and make us come to them, and we'll expend all our grenades trying to hit them. I'd rather hit what's left of them on the road, when they're more bunched together."

"I agree, partner," Tex said. "This is a better job for the citizen infantry. They'll be more effective."

"We can't guarantee no hit here," Jules said, rubbing his chin. "They try yesterday, no? They try again today or tomorrow."

"That's another thing," Ivan said, "but we can't take a request from our southern flank lightly, either. We need to work this out in detail. When are the others due back?"

"Few hours," Erica said. "Last text I got from Sam said they were following an old stagecoach road to the northeast. That's where the van tracks led them."

"Crap, that's not good," Willard said. "That road goes way out into BLM land, and ends up dangerously close to the highway."

"What highway?" Tex asked.

"Honey Springs Road," Willard said. "Which is a good route from Julian. Go south on Highway 79, make a couple transitions, and you're on that damn road."

Tex's brow furrowed. "How many hours is that?"

"Just a sec," Erica said, looking at her phone. "Hell, under two hours."

"Dammit," Ivan said.

Jules's phone dinged with a text. He read it, then hit a contact and put the phone to his ear, walking away.

"Wonder who that is?" Tex asked, "didn't like his expression."

Ivan shot a glance, his brow furrowed. Jules was back in a moment.

"I have Robbie on line. Seth and Kaitlyn's program show problem. On speaker." He set his phone down on the table and pushed the speaker button. "You hear us, Robbie?"

"Loud and clear," Robbie said. "Ben, Seth, Kaitlyn, and Morgan are here."

"Tell what see," Jules said.

Tex put his hat back on. "Yeah, partner, let us have it. We'll add it to the pile of other good news."

Sparky laughed, but then shut up when nobody else did.

"Go ahead, please," Ivan said.

"We ran the history report late this morning because of the meeting," Robbie said. "We noticed that roughly seven hundred icons disappeared."

"Uh oh," Ted said. "When?"

"Early this morning."

"From where?"

"Julian," Seth said.

"You think they're being moved in shielded vehicles?" Ted asked.

"Don't know what else to think," Seth said.

"What if they all took out their chips and burned them?" Erica asked.

"No way," Kaitlyn said. "They disappeared in a window of about ten minutes."

"I'm still not getting how they'd have the capacity to hide that many fighters," Sparky said.

"That's what we thought at first," Robbie said, "but we did some research and found out how many people could be stuffed into semi-trailers. A two-trailer semi rig could hold about five-hundred."

"Where'd you get that info?" Sparky asked.

"In an article on smuggling illegal immigrants," Kaitlyn said.

"Oh," Ivan said. "Makes sense. You're saying all they'd need is two semis to get them down here."

"That's still a lot of lead shielding," Sparky said. "Where'd they get it?"

"That's a question for another day," Ivan said. "We have to assume they solved the lead problem, and that they're coming here."

"It's likely that they're already here, partner," Tex said. "Getting pretty close to noon."

"Let's get Sam on line," Ji-Ho said.

"Yeah, I think you right," Jules said. "I patch into this call." He fumbled with his phone for a moment, then set it back down. "You on, Sam?"

"Yeah," Sam said. "Was just going to call you guys."

"Robbie, still on?" Jules asked.

"Yes," Robbie said.

"Uh oh, what's going on?" Sid asked.

Ji-Ho got closer to the phone. "History program show seven hundred enemy fighters disappear from Julian early this morning."

"Son of a bitch," Garrett said. "We're about to get hit."

"Very possible," Ivan said. "What were you guys going to tell us?"

"We're on this stagecoach road," Sid said. "All of a sudden we start seeing grayish white pebbles."

"That route the van come on?" Jules asked.

"Yes," Sid said. "There's a gravel road back here someplace."

"They probably used it to get over that dry creek bed off Honey Springs Road," Willard said. "I knew it as soon as that road got brought up."

"Who brought it up?" Garrett asked.

Willard smiled. "I did, when Erica mentioned the old stagecoach road."

"Okay, let's focus on next steps," Ivan said. "Time isn't on our side."

"I agree," Ted said. "We need to cover the back door and the front door. We know they've got at least two semis on the way."

"We don't know that for sure," Sparky said.

"Yeah, but we have to assume it," Ted said.

Jules nodded. "Ted right."

"I'm texting my guys," Garrett said. "We'll get the cannons manned and loaded. They're all pointing at the entrance roads on that side of the property. I'll get the cavalry on alert as well."

"We send off-roaders to where you are," Jules said.

"All of them?" Ted asked.

"Yes," Jules said, "off-roaders there, battle wagons here with infantry. We have many now. Enemy won't win."

"What kind of cannon do you guys have?" Ivan asked.

Seth chuckled. "Don't ask."

"Hey, don't knock them," Willard said. "They'll split a semi wide open with one shot."

Ivan's eyes were still questioning. Willard laughed. "We've got civil war cannons, sir. With plenty of powder and cannon balls. Knocked the crap out of the enemy with those suckers more than once."

"Okay, we'll chat about that later," Garrett said. "My men just got my text, and they're getting into position. Let's get those off-roaders coming this direction."

"What weapons do you guys have with you out there?" Erica asked.

"Not enough," Ed said. "Four M60s and half a dozen M4s."

"I got a crate of grenades and a mortar in the back," Sam said. "Wish we had more."

"The off-roaders will be there in hurry," Jules said. "Don't get killed. Run for it if need to. That order."

"Heard you loud and clear," Sam said. "We're in a Jeep, and we're all experienced fighters. Don't worry about us. Just get those off-roaders out here."

"Okay, we're getting off the line," Ivan said. "Good luck, all."

Jules ended the call. "To battle wagons."

"Get the women and children into the mine," Ted said.

"Well, some of the women, anyway," Erica said. "Some of us know how to fight."

"You're right about that," Tex said.

"They hit front side first," Ji-Ho said. "Try to ambush us with back people. We nail them."

"Yes, that's what I expect," Ivan said.

The group hurried out of the saloon.

***

"Mommy, where are we going?" Mia asked, as Erica rushed her to the mine, Anna following with other women and children.

"You'll take care of her?" Erica asked.

"Of course, but I wish you'd stay down here with us. We've got plenty of fighters."

"I'm one of the best," Erica said. "You know that."

Anna sighed. "I know. You've got too much of your father in you."

"Thank God for that," Erica said. They entered the dark tunnel, rushing down to one of the larger caverns, where a number of women and children were already gathered.

Kaitlyn came out when she heard them. "Are you fighting?" she asked Erica.

"Yes, but you're not," she said.

"I'm as good as you are," Kaitlyn said.

"You're better," Erica said, "only because you're younger, but that doesn't matter."

"Why not?"

"I can't write VB code. We need you down here. If not for that program you and Seth cooked up, we wouldn't have a chance."

"She's right," Seth said, head poked out of the door. "Get back in here. We've got work to do. There's plenty of people out there to fight, believe me."

Kaitlyn shrugged and shook her head. "He just doesn't want me to get hurt."

"You're damn straight," Seth said, "but the facts are the facts. We're important. We've found our niche. Our place is with the data, so come back here."

She went back into the room, turning back to Erica. "You'd better not get hurt."

"I'll do my best," she said. "At least I don't have to be in one of those tin can battle wagons."

"Mommy, I don't want you to go," Mia said, eyes brimming with tears.

"Don't worry, honey, I'll be fine," Erica said, squatting down next to her. "You stay with Auntie Anna, understand?"

"Yes, mommy," she said, looking down. "I don't want you or daddy to die."

"Don't worry," Erica said. "Neither daddy or I will die. I promise."

Anna took her hand. "Come on, Mia, let's go help the others, okay? You can be a big girl, can't you?"

She looked at Erica again, longing in her eyes, then turned to Anna and nodded yes. They disappeared into the big room, Erica looking at the empty opening for a moment, before turning and rushing outside. Her phone rang. She answered it.

"Erica?"

"Ed, what's going on. See the enemy yet?"

"No," he said. "Anna and Mia are someplace safe, right?"

"They're in the mine," she said. "I'm just leaving there now."

"Gather up some of the warriors and guard the mine," Ed said. "That's the most important thing you can do."

"I should be on the front lines," Erica said.

"I figured you'd argue. Sam, your turn."

"Hey," Sam said. "Guard Mia. Please?"

She sighed. "You two are ganging up on me."

"You're damn straight," Sam said. "It's the best place you can be. Do like Ed suggested. Lead the warriors. Protect the women and children. What could be more important than that?"

"Okay, okay, I'll do it," she said. "I'll go gather the warriors."

Sam paused for a moment. "Ed already sent them texts. They're on their way now."

Erica looked up, and saw thirty warriors rushing over, armed with M60s, RPGs, and M4s. "They're here. Talk to you later. Don't get killed."

"I won't, honey," Sam said. The call ended.

"Around the opening?" asked the first warrior.

Erica backed away from the mine, looking at the terrain and the buildings nearby. "Some on the rocks above. Some down the side street to the east. Some in that building across the road. Some in the mill on the west. Sound good?"

"Perfect," the warrior said. The men moved into position, Erica taking a place just inside the opening of the mine, where she could see the street in both directions. She checked her AK-47, then settled in to watch.

***

"Sounds like they're ready," Sid said, eyes peeled out the front of the Jeep as they rolled along the stagecoach road.

"Where's Yvonne?" Ed asked.

"She's in the battle wagon with Clem and Sarah," he said.

"Get off the road," Garrett said sharply.

Sam reacted, turning off into the weeds, on the low side of one of the hills. "What?"

"I hear a vehicle coming," he whispered as they parked.

"I hear it too," Sid said. "Quiet everybody."

"Think that's the semi?" Ryan asked.

"No, that sounds like something else," Ed said.

"The road ahead won't take a semi without some work," Garrett whispered. "There's another creek bed down at the bottom of the next valley, just over this little hill."

"We need to sneak up there and look," Sid said. "Maybe you ought to stay here and let me sneak up there. I'm good at that."

"So am I," Tyler said, "I'll join you."

"Okay, but no more," Sam said. "Don't take anything shiny up there."

Sid and Tyler both nodded, leaving the others, climbing the gentle slope of the hill, slowing when they neared the top, getting onto their bellies in the weeds.

"Glad the grass is high," Tyler whispered. Sid nodded in agreement as they inched up further.

Sid peeked over the top. "I knew it."

Tyler joined him, then both backed down.

Sam was coming up the hill to meet them on the way down. "What was it?"

"Gravel truck, filling in that creek bed," Tyler whispered.

"There isn't anywhere else that a semi can't go, until they get real close to town," Sid whispered. "We ought to wait here for them, and blast them in the valley."

"No," Sam said. "Let's backup, find some cover."

"Why?" Sid asked.

Ed chuckled. "I know why. If we take out the rig back here before their front team is in place, they'll take off, and live to fight another day with their shielded vehicle intact. We should wait until they're both committed and destroy them."

Colt Dragoon

The Jeep Unlimited drove the rutted trail in the Dodge City outback.

"We're back on my land," Garrett said. "There is a stand of trees to hide in, right where the semi will have to stop."

"How far?" Sam asked from behind the wheel.

"Couple miles," Garrett said. "There's some of my cavalry, up on that far ridge. See them?"

"Yeah," Sid said. "Surprised they didn't see the gravel."

"They don't go that far off our land," Garrett said. "We've got so much to patrol inside our own borders."

They rolled on the dusty trail, the heat of the day still rising, not enough breeze to cool them down.

Tyler took a swig from his water bottle, then wiped sweat off his brow. "We got enough coverage for the town with all the off-roaders coming here?"

"Should," Sam said. "We've got all those battle wagons."

"Hell of a lot of infantry now, too," Garrett said. "I'd be a lot more worried if it was just our original group."

"Seriously," Ed said. "Wish I was gonna be there for the cannon fire."

Garrett chuckled. "Yeah, those old cannon do get your blood up."

"Wait till you hear the microguns on the off-roaders," Ryan said. "Looked up some video. They're so fast they hardly sound like guns."

"Why did they kill that program?" Sid asked.

"Yeah, good question," Ed said.

Sam smiled. "I never saw the official reason, but I can guess."

"Let's have it," Garrett said.

"They're too heavy to carry, so they've got to be mounted on a vehicle. The difference in weight and ammo storage space from the next size up doesn't make enough difference to the army. They'd rather have twenty extra pounds and the higher power of the larger rounds."

"Ah, but we've got an application that can take advantage, where the size and weight does make a difference," Tyler said.

"Yep, the army didn't have off-roaders," Sam said. "Seems like a pretty good fit to me."

"Is that the stand of trees you're talking about?" Sid asked, pointing ahead.

"Yep," Garrett said. "The semi can't get through the rocky pass that's right beyond there."

"Yeah, I remember that," Sid said. "The enemy van could get by, but just barely."

The Jeep sped up on the flat section of road heading to the small tree-covered ridge.

"This is perfect," Sam said. "There's more of your mounted guys, Garrett."

"They're all over the place, and we'll need them," Garrett said. "When we break open that semi there'll be a lot of enemy fighters on foot."

"Unless we can land a mortar round on them before they get out," Sid said.

"I don't think we can count on that much luck," Ed said. "If these microguns can get through the sides, that might do a lot of damage."

"Wonder how they'll do getting through lead lining?" Tyler asked.

"Probably not good enough," Sam said. "We'll need our men with M60s to punch through."

Garrett chuckled. "Lots of my cavalry guys have .50 caliber plains rifles. They don't have a high rate of fire, but when you've got over a hundred men with them, they can turn things into swiss cheese in a hurry."

The Jeep pulled past the stand of trees, parking back far enough to be out of sight.

"Here we are," Garrett said. "Let's fan out wide."

"Think they know how far in they can get?" Ryan asked.

"I'm sure they do," Sam said. "They knew enough to drop gravel in specific locations. They know how far their semi-trucks can go too. Their van team saw it. I'm sure they were in constant contact with the base."

"We have to assume that," Ed said.

The men got out with their weapons, Sam going to the back to get the mortar and grenades.

"Want some help with that?" Ed asked.

"Sure," Sam said. "Don't know how much good this mortar will be, but it's worth trying."

"Listen," Ryan said. "I hear off-roaders."

"Here they come," Tyler said. "Those things are so bitchen." The small vehicles came forward from the rocky pass, fanning out in the stand of trees.

"I want one," Ryan said.

Sam left Ed to the mortar and rushed over to talk to the lead rider, while Sid and Garrett picked out spots for sniping at the enemy.

Sam trotted over to them.

"What'd you tell them?" Garrett asked.

"I told them to stay out of sight until we start shooting," Sam said, "and for them to concentrate fire with the grenades first, then move to the microguns after the sides of the semi-trailers have been breached, and the fighters are getting out."

"Who's sending us the word from town?" Sid asked.

Sam chuckled. "Everybody and their brother."

"Won't even matter," Ed said, walking over. "We'll know the other attack is happening when they open the semi-trailers. We'll all get buzzed when the chips are exposed."

"You're right," Sid said. "Hell, we'll probably hear the gunfire."

"Time to wait," Garrett said, pulling his phone out. He sent a text to his forces, in the outback and in town.

***

Trevor and Kaylee drove their battle wagon into position, behind an old barn situated on the road into town.

"Good, I can see my uncle from here," Kaylee said. "Glad he upgraded from the prototype. These new rigs can take a lot more damage."

"Yeah," Trevor said, "and they've got more firepower, too, with the grenade launcher. Who's with him?"

"Clem, Sarah, and Yvonne. Wish they had somebody younger with them, though."

"Hope they don't have Ivan in one of these things," Trevor said. "There's Angel and Megan's rig, see it? Just past the mill."

"Glad Kaitlyn and Seth are staying in the mine," Kaylee said.

"Does Kaitlyn mind? I know she's one of the best. She prides herself on that."

"Megan said she argued a little, but Erica helped convince her."

Trevor smiled. "I suspect Seth had something to do with that as well."

Kaylee laughed. "Look at Willard, over there with that row of cannons. Is that a civil war cap he's got on?"

Trevor looked at him and cracked up. "Yep. At least it's a Union cap."

Suddenly there was a pop and an explosion, some forty yards from where they were.

"They've got mortars set up off the property," Trevor said, sending a text. "They're gonna soften us up before they bring in their rig. Should've thought about that."

"There goes Ted's coach," Kaylee said, watching as the battle wagon raced towards the front end of the property. It stopped, the grenade launcher firing in the direction of the mortar fire. Another mortar round dropped, closer to them by about twenty yards.

"We'd better not stay here," Trevor said, starting the engine. He drove forward on the road, firing grenades as well, several other battle wagons roaring forward, doing the same. Then a hail of gunfire sounded, black powder smoke rising from trees along the highway, three hundred yards from their position. Ted's battle wagon got closer, opening up with the mini gun, the stream of bullets chopping through tree branches, setting off a secondary explosion. Then another mortar round went off, past them this time but coming from another direction, getting nearly to the first buildings in town.

"Crap," Kaylee yelled.

"I think the cannon team on the right sees where that's coming from," Trevor said, watching six men working the gun, turning it towards the right. Then it fired, the sound ear-shattering, a secondary explosion going off four hundred yards away. The team struggled to get the big gun loaded again as AK-47 fire came at them, dropping a couple of the team.

"Whoa, here comes the semi-truck," Kaylee said. She leveled the front machine guns and fired as it approached, hitting the driver and passenger, as several other battle wagons opened up on it. Then the cannons on the left side fired at once, cannon balls ripping into the trailer.

"My phone buzzed," Trevor said. "They lost their shield."

"Yeah, mine buzzed too," Kaylee shouted. "Look at them flooding out of there!"

"They're getting into that cover before Ted can hit them," Trevor said, firing his mini gun through the cab, into the front of the trailer, as another volley of cannon fire hit it broadside, blowing it off its wheels, Islamists fleeing right into the infantry, hit with a hail of lead.

"The guys in that busted trailer are still getting out," Kaylee said. "The lead inside must soak up bullets pretty well. I can't hit them from here." She froze. "Look at those guys with the mortars."

"See them," Trevor said, opening fire with the mini gun, knocking them down, another group of men rushing forward, trying to get the mortars into the dry creek bed, giving them some cover. More infantry rushed in, and then the cavalry was everywhere, chasing down fleeing Islamists, hitting them with pistol fire and swords, newer recruits rushing forward with their M4s and M60s.

"Look at that group, coming through the brush over there," Kaylee yelled. "Looks like UN Peacekeepers from outside the property. Hit them, they're heading for town."

Trevor nodded, firing several grenades in their direction, pinning them down, then moving to the mini gun as Ji-Ho's battle wagon moved in that direction. A group of Islamists charged towards it, but then the gun slit opened, an M60 firing, cutting down the rushing men, killing most, causing the rest to retreat. Soon that area was filled with cavalry, chasing Islamists into the trees, terrorizing them with their swords and pistols, some men shooting Winchesters one handed, causing Trevor to crack up.

"What's funny about this?" Kaylee asked, looking up from her target reticle.

"The guy at the gun range," Trevor said, "warned us against using our Winchesters like that. Works pretty damn good, from the look of it."

"Look out, we're getting rushed broadside," Kaylee shouted.

"Too close for the mini gun," Trevor said, rushing to the back and opening the gun slit, firing the M60, taking down six, the rest running for their lives. As soon as they were far enough out, Kaylee opened up with the mini gun, cutting them to ribbons. "Nice shooting, baby!"

"They've got more people than we expected," Kaylee shouted. "Look at all those UN Peacekeepers over there. My uncle is gonna get overrun."

"No he's not, look. Ted's rig is moving there, and Cody's, and Jules's." They watched as fire from four mini guns tore the UN Peacekeepers apart.

"Geez," Kaylee said. "This is insane."

The cannons fired again, Trevor's head snapping around. "Dammit, that's another semi. Does this mean they're not coming in through the back as well?"

"Texting Seth," Kaylee said. "Keep on those guys."

Trevor rushed to the front, getting back on the main guns, firing grenades at the new semi, just as a salvo of cannon fire slammed into the trailer, their phones buzzing with new enemy hits. "Can't stop long enough to look."

"Seth said there's a total of seven hundred and forty-five," Kaylee said. "They've dropped about four hundred and fifty here. There's three hundred exposed in the back as we speak."

"I think there's been about two hundred UN Peacekeepers here, too, although Ji-Ho, Ted, Cody, and some of the new folks blasted their asses good."

"There's too many of them," Kaylee said, blasting a group rushing up from behind with the rear machine guns.

"They're really flooding out of that semi-trailer, but I can't get a clear shot from here," Trevor said. Just then the cannons fired again, picking up the trailer, rolling it over a large group of fleeing Islamists. "Ouch, that's gotta hurt."

"Hit them," Kaylee shouted, getting on her forward machine guns again and firing at those she could target. Trevor was back on the mini gun, firing away, until the gun spun silently.

"Out of ammo, switching to the grenade launcher."

"I'll use the grenade launcher, you go reload," Kaylee said.

"Okay." Trevor rushed to the bedroom as Kaylee took over the targeting system, firing grenade after grenade into the enemy cover, behind the burning hulk of a semi-truck. The cannons fired again, moving the hulk over, more of Garrett's infantry rushing in with guns blazing.

"Reloaded," Trevor said, rushing back to the front. As he got back into the driver's seat there was a mortar hit about twenty feet from their rig, shrapnel splattering against the passenger side, right front tire going soft.

"Dammit, we're hit," Kaylee said.

"It's okay, we didn't get breached," Trevor said, firing up the engine.

"What are you doing?"

"Using the levelers so we're sitting straight again," he said. Then there was a loud explosion on the roof behind them, shaking the rig, their ears ringing.

"We'd better get out of here," Kaylee shouted, going for her M4.

"Yep," Trevor shouted back, grabbing his M60 and two belts, slinging his Winchester on his shoulder, grabbing boxes of ammo and stuffing them into his pockets. "Me first."

Kaylee nodded as Trevor rushed to the door, bursting through it, seeing enemy fighters heading toward them, opening up with the M60, cutting them down before they could get off a shot. He rushed out, taking Kaylee's hand, both running into the small barn they'd been parked behind.

"Hey, this is better," Trevor said, leveling the M60 and firing at a group of Islamists who were attempting to set up another mortar, spraying them with lead, concentrating next on the box of rounds, which blew up big. "Take that, you cretins!"

"Watch out," Kaylee shouted, firing her M4 at a group of Islamists running in from the left. Trevor saw them, dropping the M60 and bringing up the Winchester, firing shot after shot, dropping somebody with each, then getting up and running towards the survivors, hitting them as they ran in a panic. He turned and sprinted back into the barn, leaping through the door, stuffing more .44 mag rounds into the loading gate of the rifle.

Kaylee looked at him like he was crazy. "Quit showing off, dammit."

"I wasn't showing off, I knew they'd flee, and I can't run with that damn M60. Hell, that thing will be out of ammo soon, the way it fires."

Kaylee shook her head, watching for more enemy fighters approaching. "I don't think they want to come back this way."

"Then we'll just have to go get them," Trevor said. "See that group over there? They're trying to go after the cannon team. I'll be damned if I'm letting Willard get tagged."

"You're enjoying this a little too much, honey," she said, following him as he sprinted across the pasture towards the trees lining the dry creek, firing the Winchester as he got close, killing most of the Islamists there, Kaylee getting down on one knee and cleaning them up with the M4. Willard saw them and grinned, then noticed an Islamist charging him, firing his cap and ball revolver, throwing the man ten feet, the smoke billowing around him.

"Settled his bacon!" Willard shouted.

"What the hell was that?" Kaylee asked. "You see how far it threw that guy?"

"Looks like a Colt Dragoon to me," Trevor said, twinkle in his eye. "Come on. Let's go hunt some more heathens."

They rushed out of their cover, sprinting by the cannon team who let out a cheer, running down the dry lake bed, catching several Islamists trying to escape in that direction. Trevor got off two shots, but then they were around a bend, getting too far ahead. "Those cowards run pretty fast."

"Yeah," Kaylee said, trying to catch her breath. Then they heard automatic fire ahead, and the Islamists rushed back at them, Trevor laughing and opening fire, Kaylee joining in, killing eight of them before they could find their way to cover.

"Let's stop a minute and check the apps," Kaylee said, leaning against the cover of the creek bed, Trevor next to her, eyes scanning in all directions with the Winchester in his hands. "There's someone moving over there, trying to sneak into the main street."

"I wouldn't suggest that," Trevor said. "I saw where Erica was placing the warriors earlier. She started out just setting up a defense for the mine, but when everybody saw how good she was at that, they had her work out defense for the entire town. It's a kill zone."

"We should still try to get them first, though, right?"

"We'll go hit some of them, and get them running that way. Text Erica and tell her to get ready."

"Like I said, you're enjoying this too much," Kaylee said.

"It's almost over. Gunfire is way down, and there's not a bunch more coming, right?"

"Doesn't look like it, but maybe they have more shielded vehicles."

"Let's go," Trevor said, rushing forward through the tall grass of the pasture, firing from behind the group of twenty Islamists as they rushed towards Main Street, hitting several of them, causing the rest to sprint down the road in a panic. Then there was a barrage of automatic fire, a few of the Islamists trying to flee back, running right into Trevor and Kaylee's guns, all of them blown away before they could get close.

The cannons fired once again, and gunfire behind them ramped up. Both of them got buzzed by their phones.

"Dammit, more? Kaylee asked, looking at Trevor in horror. "We're gonna run out of ammo if this keeps up."

"We've got plenty, but we'll have to take it from the mine," Trevor said. "Better go get my M60. They rushed back to the barn, going in the back as bullets hit the old wood structure, both diving to the straw-covered floor, Trevor getting to the M60. He rolled over, opening fire at the men sprinting towards them, cutting down a bunch. Then the firing stopped. "Dammit, got to load a new belt."

"I'll cover, Kaylee said, firing her M4, keeping the enemy down, watching as they crawled along the ground toward them.

"Got it," Trevor said, crawling forward, sweeping M60 fire along the dirt, hitting about half of them, the others rolling away as quickly as they could, Trevor switching to the Winchester to pick them off as they rushed for cover.

Gunfire was back up to a fever pitch now, the battle wagons mostly silent, but the infantry and cavalry fighting off the enemy valiantly.

"What happened to the cannon?" Kaylee asked. "We need to blast open that semi-trailer so they can't hide in it."

"Got overrun," Trevor said. "Hope the hell Willard got away from there before it happened.

Kaylee crawled over. "Crap, look, the enemy are still there, trying to figure out if they can do something."

"Oh, really?" Trevor asked. He crawled over. "See that barrel?"

"What barrel?"

Trevor fired at it, the black powder inside blowing up big, several men flying through the air. "That barrel!"

Somebody rushed in behind them, Trevor spinning around, Winchester pointed.

"Don't shoot, it's me, Willard!" he said, diving to the ground with his heavy Colt Dragoon in his hand.

"Willard, what the hell happened out there?" Trevor asked.

"They finally got the drop on us. Killed several. We're in trouble."

"What kind of trouble?" Kaylee asked.

"There's two more of those semi-trucks out there, waiting to come in, and we need a little time to reload. That's why those battle wagons haven't been firing. They're mostly out of ammo."

"We have more, though," Trevor said.

"Yeah, in the mine we got lots," Willard said. "We need to get it to the others, though. Your battle wagon still working?"

"Nope, got damaged," Trevor said.

"So did some of the others," Willard said. "They can still fire, but three of them got their tires shot all to hell."

"Couldn't stay in siege mode because they kept having to move around," Trevor said. "That's what happened with us."

"Seth's program is missing things," Kaylee said, looking at her phone as the gunfire raged outside. "There's more than seven hundred enemy fighters out here now, and that's not even counting the ones who came in the back."

"Probably not counting the two still on the road, neither," Willard said.

"Crap, we need to think," Trevor said.

"There's still some un-used battle wagons in town," Willard said. "How come we didn't use them?"

"Didn't have enough folks to man them," Trevor said. "Remember we weren't expecting to be attacked so soon. We got about an hour notice, and these rigs take some training."

Kaylee smiled. "Wonder if the keys are in them? We can ferry ammo and attack."

They got buzzed on their phones. "Dammit, enemy fighters getting out of one of the trucks," Trevor said.

Kaylee nodded, brow furrowed. "We're gonna get overrun."

To be continued, in Bug Out! California Book 10…

Cast Of Characters

Note: some of these characters are not in the first book. They will show up later in the story.

Dulzura RV Park Group – Mostly retired people, but mixed. Full-timers.

John – Older man, drinking problem, but fighting it. Brave and strong.

Sarah – John's wife. Doesn't his like drinking, but loyal any-way. Good heart.

Clem – Old widower. Shrewd with sense of humor, and technically savvy.

Sid – Indian, capable, good man in fight, loyal, cunning.

Yvonne – Sid's wife. Resourceful and brave. Younger than him by ten years

Harry – Older man, heavy, doesn't move well, good negotiator and strategist.

Nancy – Harry's wife, retired school teacher. Smart but has problems with stress.

Sam – Owner of RV Park. Middle aged, strong, wily, cautious. Former Navy Seal with some PTSD issues, which he has mostly under control. Good in a fight, knows modern military tactics and weapons systems.

Connie – Wife of Sam. Thinks one step ahead. Keeps park running. Deeply in love with Sam.

CHP Officer Ryan – Older officer. Brave, sense of humor, borderline redneck, good in fight, but has temper.

CHP Officer Patrick – Just past rookie status. Extremely good with guns. A little green. A little hapless. Good in fight. Brave to a fault.

Jack, aka One Eye – Barona Indian, friend of Sid's who helps at the battle of Fernbrook.

Hank – police officer in the town of Julian. Older man, gray hair, feisty. Joins group after they destroy the enemy checkpoint in his town. Works with Jason.

Jason – police officer in town of Julian. Younger, fast with a gun, smart as a whip. Aggressive. Joins group after they destroy the enemy checkpoint in his town. Works with Hank.

Kaitlyn aka Still Pool – young woman in Barona Tribe. Curvy, pretty face, strong personality. Goes after what she wants, loyal and passionate, smart.

Megan aka Sage Flower – young woman in Barona Tribe. Tiny, delicate beauty, feisty, loud, aggressive, brave, smart. Wicked sense of humor.

Zac aka Sandy Creek - young Indian warrior. Brave and handsome, cunning.

James aka Crossbow – young Indian warrior, expert with weapons, especially crossbows. Brave, funny sense of humor, loved by the tribe.

Ryan aka Touchdown – young Indian warrior, brave, fast, CIF MVP in High School, great in a fight.

Tyler aka Quiet Fox – young Indian Warrior, smart, thinks a couple levels deep, quiet, reserved, observes and thinks before acting, usually makes right choice. Future Chief.

Nurse Grace – Emergency room nurse, taking care of Sam and Connie at the hospital in La Quinta. Pretty middle-aged woman, tough as nails and smart as a whip.

Kenny – warrior with the Barona Tribe.

Bradley – warrior with the Barona Tribe.

Silver Wolf – overall chief of the Barona Tribe. Older man, medium build, looks younger than his years. Total tech nut, very talented and inventive.

Kerry aka Yellow Bird – young warrior. Fast, too emotional. Unpredictable.

Shane aka Red Snake – warrior, a little older, family man but also great fighter.

Will aka Swimming Bear – warrior, early thirties, negotiator, helps Silver Wolf with technology.

Mia – wife of Tyler. Strong, beautiful, smart. Delicate features, hair-trigger emotions.

Riley – wife of Ryan. Very small, below five feet tall. Beautiful face. Has Ryan wrapped around her finger.

Abby – wife of James – heavy set larger woman with an infectious smile and a gentle, kind way about her. Beautiful face.

Redondo Condo group – Thirty-something

Robbie – Thirty-something son of Frank and Jane from original series. Brave, thoughtful, writer, shy, cynical

Morgan – neighbor of Robbie, love interest. Strong, more out-going and aggressive than Robbie, pretty, transplant from Utah, good with guns.

Gil – Robbie's best friend from High School. Hispanic. Good with guns, brave, sense of humor, cautious, protective.

Steve – Robbie's friend from college. Smart but not serious, surfer, scrappy, good in fight

Justin – Robbie's friend from high school and college. Sparks with others, temper, suspicious nature but good heart

Killer – Pit Bull – from Justin's family. Strong, protective, dangerous to evil-doers.

Colleen – girlfriend of Steve. Beautiful redhead. Flighty, aggressive, but loyal and loving.

Katie – Steve's sister. Strong, rebellious, great in a fight, beautiful. Justin adores her. She brings out his courage.

Cody – neighbor who lives across the street from Frank and Jane's Condo. Friends with them. Tough reserve police officer and early resistance fighter. Large muscular man in his early thirties with a military style haircut, light brown hair, and a goatee.

Sparky – Morgan's boss at the card club. Big, dangerous man with a shady past but a good heart. Protects his employees to a fault. Has underworld connections. Not a good person to mess with.

Ivan the Butcher – mob boss. Most people assume he's from Russia, but he's actually an American who built his organization in Russia and Europe, before being hounded back home by the EU authorities. Dangerous and unpredictable, but a strategic thinker. Childhood friend of Sparky.

Jules – right hand man of Ivan the Butcher. Belgian national, good in a fight, a little crazy but very calculating.

Tex – Friend of Sparky and Jules. Crazy with wicked sense of humor, great in a fight, brave to a fault.

Ted – Robbie's boss at the restaurant. Former Navy Seal, tricked into joining the battle by Sparky. Old friends with Ivan the Butcher.

Bryan – cook in Ted's restaurant, acquaintance of Robbie's. Heavy-set large man, good in a fight, not the brightest but loyal and brave to a fault.

Jordan – black man, former Army Ranger. Near genius tactical expert. Brave and cunning, trusts nobody until he's sure, then as loyal as the day is long. Wicked sense of humor.

Dana – beautiful girl who was kidnapped by the UN to use as a sex slave. Rescued by Jules's team after the battle at Torrance Civic Center.

Karen – beautiful redhead, daughter of Gil's boss. Captured and held at the Torrance Police Station with the other girls. Not sure where she fits in the group.

Tisha – wild young woman, former captive. Small, tattooed and pierced, fiery, hard to handle, brave and loyal but prickly. Passionate.

Alexis - a brunette with a hauntingly beautiful face and a thin build. Tough and loyal but with a sadness in her that she battles constantly. Valuable member of the team.

Brooke - tall, dark haired beauty with a strong build and a defensive demeanor. Lesbian. Protective of her woman. Fierce, loyal fighter. Touchy but with a good heart. Smart.

Audrey – Doctor. Lesbian, close to Brooke. A small waif with ginger hair and freckles.

Lily – a small blonde, willowy, with a delicate face. Has emotional issues. Bipolar. Suicidal. Barely survived captivity.

Shelly – short, perky blonde with a beautiful face and a way with organization. Valuable member of the team.

Ashley - Curly-haired brunette with a dancer's body and grace, with a quiet demeanor. Not sure she's up to the fight, but feels it's her duty. Likes Jordan, because they both have the theater bug.

Brianna - a young-looking girl with an innocent face and curly light brown hair. Not very confident. Frightened by the war. Bryan is pursuing her, and she's okay with it, but not passionate.

Haley - an ice blond with a curvy figure and a lot of self-confidence. Good fighter.

Allison - a redhead of medium build. She has a country look to her, innocent but with a touch of mischief. Expert hunter and backpacker, champion level shooter. Ready for anything. Will become a principle in the group over time.

South Torrance Group – Ages from 19 to 24. Well-to-do parents. Some recently on their own, some live with parents. Gun hobbyists. Immature but with enthusiasm.

Seth – defacto leader of group due to calm, easy going nature mixed with charisma. Gets along with everybody in group. Slightly more mature than the others. Has serious girlfriend, centers his life around her, in love.

Emma – Seth's girlfriend. Beautiful, was popular in high school, aggressive, controlling, but nice, loyal. Needs Seth when she gets scared or upset. Doesn't like Matt or Trevor much. Feeling is mutual. Likes Angel.

Trevor – talented, brilliant, great with guns, nutty, good sense of humor. Aggressive with temper. Likes to argue. Younger than the others by a year. Came into group as Seth's friend, closest to him.

Angel – cynical sense of humor, honest and trustworthy. His-panic. Lives with family, but inching out. Good in fight. Seth's best friend. Pivotal member of group, head for business and practicality. Slightly more mature than the others.

Matt – Angel's oldest friend. Funny, problems with drinking, emotional, secondary leader who sparks with Seth sometimes, but they are close in ways the others aren't. Good in fight, image is important to him, womanizer. Has serious girlfriend but cheats on her.

Kaylee – Matt's girlfriend. Nice, talented, good friend of Em-ma, clueless about Matt's infidelity, doesn't like him drinking, get-ting tired of his childish behavior. Beautiful in an exotic way, Korean.

Ji-Ho – Kaylee's rich uncle, lives in compound on north-west side of Palos Verdes, overlooking ocean. Brave and smart, loyal, understands what it's like when government gets too much control. Can relate well to younger people, even though his English isn't great.

Gus – combat tactics trainer, met group at gun range. Great organizer and leader. Serious. Destined for greatness if he lives long enough.

Government/Authorities

Governor Sable – fourth-term governor of California. Old-style liberal – coming to the conclusion that there really is something wrong with the Administration. Knows how to do the right thing, and usually does after fits and starts. Watch out when he gets angry.

Jennifer – Sable's black secretary. They were lovers years ago, now friends, but Nancy keeps her distance because Sable still loves her. Competent and smart – Sable's underground advisor.

Saladin – evil Islamic leader, trying to move the US towards martial law with terror attacks. Acting in collusion with the President and others. Kills without mercy or regard for innocent by-standers. Pretends to be pious, but only uses his religion to gain power. Human trash.

Commissioner Frawley – head of CHP for California. Currently in prison after going against the Governor and the Administration. Strong character, brave, will make difference.

Deputy Commissioner Katz – second in command at CHP – al-so in prison. Hates Jihadists. Dangerous man to his enemies. Near-genius intelligence.

Assistant Commissioner Cooley – third in command at CHP, in prison with other two commissioners. Black man. Brave, strong, emotional, smart. Always has your back. Wicked sense of humor.

Chief Smith – turncoat chief of CHP – helped capture the commissioners. No stomach for violence. A coward, only in his position because he's related to Sable. Follows whoever he's most scared of at any given time. Trusts nobody, in it for himself.

President Simpson – ineffective, corrupt leader of the United States. In league with the enemy.

Attorney General Blake – Simpson's right-hand man. Corrupt and evil.